CHRISTOS IKONOMOU

Something Will Happen, You'll See

Translated from Greek by Karen Emmerich

archipelago books

Archipelago Books
232 3rd Street #A111
Brooklyn, NY 11215
www.archipelagobooks.org

Library of Congress Cataloging-in-Publication Data
Names: Oikonomou, Chråestos, 1970– author. | Emmerich, Karen, translator.
Title: Something will happen, you'll see / by Christos Ikonomou ; translated
    from Greek by Karen Emmerich.
Description: 1st Archipelago Books edition, 2016. | Brooklyn, NY :
    Archipelago Books, [2016]
Identifiers: LCCN 2015035558
Classification: LCC PA5638.25.I37 A2 2016 | DDC 889.3/4—dc23
LC record available at http://lccn.loc.gov/2015035558

Distributed by Penguin Random House
www.penguinrandomhouse.com

Cover art by Joseph Beuys

This publication was made possible with support from the Onassis Foundation, Lannan
Foundation, the New York State Council on the Arts, a state agency, the New York City
Department of Cultural Affairs, and the National Endowment for the Arts.

PRINTED IN THE UNITED STATES OF AMERICA

To Julia

Something Will Happen, You'll See

Come on Ellie, Feed the Pig

SHE'S WASHING LETTUCE. With twenty euros to get her through the week and bills piled on the kitchen counter. But it's Friday night, her favorite night of the week, and Ellie Drakou is at the sink washing lettuce which she likes because it has such a tender white heart. She pulls off each leaf individually and runs water over it and washes it carefully and strokes it and breaks off any rotten edges or pieces with those strange tiny brown holes that lettuce gets and then gently shakes off the water and lays the leaf in the basin.

She loves washing lettuce. Pulling off those big green leaves and washing each one individually. And as she gets closer to the center she reaches those tender leaves that are less green, the ones that glisten like they're untouched by time. It's as if she's slowly and carefully and excitedly unwrapping a gift that someone else wrapped in layers of green paper. Then she gets to the heart of the lettuce and her own heart sweetens at the sight of those small tender leaves, those white crispy leaves – the heart of a head of lettuce, a tiny miracle, a well-kept secret, guarded from time and the wear of time. She likes to think that no matter what happened yesterday, no matter how much money she may have lost, no matter what happens tomorrow and for the rest of her days, no matter how many Sotirises pass through her life like conquering soldiers or hunted migrants, the heart of the lettuce, the innermost heart of the lettuce, those tiny leaves now quivering in her wet hands will remain forever white and tender and alive, as if they're the only things in this world that don't die, that won't ever die.

It rained, then stopped. Soon it will rain again. She looks out the window. Everything to the west is red – wind, sky, clouds. Tonight it'll rain blood, Ellie says and shivers. And her eyes move from the window back to the heart of the lettuce that seems to be throbbing in her hands – but it's not the lettuce that's throbbing, only her hands trembling – and what she sees sinks inside of her like the smile of a person who's out of work, a person who's just been fired.

. . .

Lettuce, says Ellie. The whole secret of life hiding in a head of lettuce. Am I right?

. . .

She was the only one who fed the pig. For the past ten months or even a year. Every other day, sometimes every day. A euro or two euros or sometimes five. Occasionally she forgot. She forgot when she'd been working overtime and came home so tired she couldn't even speak. But Sotiris never forgot. He would bring the pig in from the kitchen – it was big and heavy and pink with a slit in its back for coins and a hole in its snout for bills – and shake it in front of Ellie's face.

Grrts grrts. The pig is hungry. It's starving, Ellie. Grrts grrts. Come on Ellie, feed the pig. Don't you feel sorry for the poor thing? Grrts grrts.

And Ellie would laugh. No matter how exhausted she was she always laughed. And she would open her wallet and take out a euro or two and slip the coin into the hole and on Friday nights she would take a five-euro bill out of her wallet and twist it into a tight roll and push it through the pig's snout.

There must have been about eight hundred in there. Eight or maybe nine at the very most.

Why don't you ever feed it, she sometimes asked. Why don't you feed it every now and then, why do you just wait for me to?

Wheatie. That's what she called him sometimes, wheatie instead of sweetie, because everything about him was the color of wheat. Wheat-colored skin, wheat-colored hair, even his eyes were the color of wheat. Wheat or semolina. I want to eat you with a spoon. You'll just lie there as still as can be and I'll eat you one spoonful at a time all night long. And in the morning you'll be whole and I'll eat you up all over again.

Like wheat. Like semolina.

Whatever you say, he told her, I won't spoil your fun.

He came over with the pig in his hands.

It won't eat my money, he said. You've spoiled it. It's a gourmet pig it won't eat just anything. It won't eat dirty money.

He worked at a gas station on Thebes Street and his hands were always grimy. The tops of his fingernails were like black half-moons. Black half-moons, little black scythes.

. . .

She washes the last leaf and puts it in the basin and sets the basin aside for later. Later she might fix a salad with lots of dill and onion and throw in some cold rice and a little tuna from the jar a girl at work brought her, a jar of tuna from Alonissos which she's been eating for a month now in tiny little bites one flake at a time – Sotiris didn't like it, he thought it was too fishy.

The bills are piled on the kitchen counter. On the very top is the phone bill, which is ten days overdue and yesterday or the day before they cut off her line.

She opens the fridge to see if there's something sweet she can eat. Her hands are trembling again. Low blood sugar for sure. Chocolates. She still remembers those chocolates someone once brought her from France. See what it's like when you've got a good man, Sotiris said. See. Everyone remembers to bring you something. They ate one each night. Only one because it wasn't a very big box. The brand was named after some queen or princess who had lived a long long time ago in England and once begged her husband the king to abolish the taxes he'd levied on the poor and he agreed on the condition that the queen ride her horse naked through the city streets and she also agreed on the condition that everyone lock themselves in their houses so no one would see and she rode the horse naked through the streets hiding her nakedness with her long long hair and everyone stayed locked in their houses except for a single man who supposedly dared to sneak a peek at her and was immediately struck blind.

Ellie had told that story to Sotiris two or three times, and she'd told it many more to herself, and each time she tried to imagine what the queen looked like and if she had blonde hair or black and why the queen cared about poor people and if she had ridden the horse the way men do or if she sat sidesaddle and what she was thinking as she passed naked through the empty streets and if it was day or night and how slowly she rode – and now, as she stands in front of the empty fridge with the cold hitting her face, Ellie remembers those summer evenings in bed remembers unwrapping the chocolate and holding it between two fingers and licking it a little before putting it in her mouth and when she put it in her mouth she didn't bite it but let it melt on her tongue, didn't bite didn't chew but let the chocolate slowly melt in her mouth and the sweet and bitter taste would coat her mouth and run down her throat and into her heart.

. . .

Chains, Ellie says and closes the door of the fridge and rubs her arms which are covered in gooseflesh. I should put snow chains on my mind to keep it from slipping back to the past.

. . .

In the bathroom she looks again at the word scrawled in orange lipstick on the mirror. *THORRY*. It was one of their jokes, their secret phrases. They'd stolen it from a movie they saw on TV, about a clumsy guy with a lisp who was always eating chocolate and apologizing to everyone. Thorry, he kept saying, excthuse me.

Thorry, Sotiris would say to Ellie. A woman like you should have found a rich guy to be with. Then you wouldn't have to work the way you do. You would just travel and shop and go to the hair salon. Rome for the weekend Paris on Monday holidays in New York. But then I had to come along. Thorry.

THORRY is what Sotiris had scrawled last night on the bathroom mirror with her orange lipstick.

. . .

She turns on the cold tap and holds her breath and steps into the bathtub under the water tensing her whole body so she won't scream. The water falls hard on her skin like blades slicing her to pieces – but Ellie tells herself she can stand it and tries to ignore the pain and blinks and sees images passing in front of her eyes like ghosts born of the running water and her running brain sees faces and landscapes and mornings and nights passing in front of her eyes sees images from another life another era when there were no factories no overtime no punching a clock no unpaid bills or pigs that needed feeding or men who ran off like thieves in the night.

Under the icy water the color of her skin changes, the pallid color seems to fall from her skin like old whitewash chipping off a wall. Her breasts harden and rise like a fox's snout in the bushes. Ellie strokes her chest and feels panicked blood coursing through her body and she rubs her petrified belly and wiggles her toes and watches drops of water fall on her peeling toenails.

My toenails, says Ellie. The southernmost border of my body. Where my body ends, where Ellie ends, where the nation of Ellie ends.

Not much of a border. It might as well be a strainer, I might as well hang a sign that says come on in make yourselves at home.

The Unguarded Democracy of Ellie.

. . .

In the bedroom she puts on her old lilac bathrobe and lights a cigarette then pads barefoot into the kitchen and thinks about unplugging the telephone but the line's been cut so there would be no point.

She pours a glass of wine – dark red Cretan wine almost black like old blood – and as she pours it into the glass she sees her hands shaking and thinks how she really needs to eat something sweet, that's the problem for sure, low blood sugar.

She smokes and drinks and when she's through with her cigarette she goes back into the bedroom and opens the closet and pulls all his clothes off the hangers and tosses them in a big ball onto the unmade bed. Shirts, pants, a cheap fake fur coat, an old suit. She pulls out all the drawers and empties them onto the bed. Underwear, socks, a twisted tie. A belt with a broken buckle. An insole for a size 45 shoe. A long yellow shoelace. At the top of the pile she puts his shoes and slippers.

On the way to the bathroom she stops in the kitchen to light another cigarette and refill her glass. Then she goes into the bathroom which is the most difficult part of the house because it's where people leave the most complicated traces. She opens the medicine cabinet and tosses his razors onto the floor and his cologne and comb and nail clipper. A bottle of rubbing alcohol. His scissors.

And that little brush she'd bought for him so he could scrub the grime from under his nails after work.

In the living room she sweeps up whatever she finds in her path. Sports papers and car magazines and lighters and empty cigarette packs and old photographs. His things. All his things, scattered through the apartment like crumbs.

In the cupboard under the sink she finds green trash bags that cinch with a yellow plastic ribbon. She bags up Sotiris's clothes and all the rest of his things and drags the bags over to the balcony door. Outside it's stopped raining but drops of water are still dripping from the balcony railing and Ellie stands and watches them – just look at that, Ellie says, tonight even the metal bars are crying.

She lights a cigarette and a cough climbs up her throat so that she can't breathe.

For the money, Ellie says. All that for a handful of money.

She opens the door, coughing, and goes out onto the balcony. She grabs a garbage bag from inside and throws it over the railing into the street. She hears the thump but doesn't look down. She throws another bag and then another. The drivers on the street slow down and raise their heads. One man out walking his dog stops and looks up. Garbage bags are falling from the sky at the corner of Cyprus and Ionia Streets in Nikaia – garbage bags are falling from the third floor like suicidal women in green dresses, like cowardly sinners on the night when the end of the world will come.

The man bends down and hefts his dog into his arms and runs off without looking back.

Just think, he even took the pig, Ellie says. The pig.

. . .

Ellie goes back into the kitchen. Her hands are still shaking, they're shaking even more now. It's low blood sugar for sure. She opens drawers and cupboards and lines up semolina and sugar and honey and almonds and cinnamon on the counter. She'll make halva. A nice semolina halva with almonds and plenty of cinnamon. It's low blood sugar for sure.

She puts the almonds on to boil and tries to remember the recipe, how the proportions go. One two three four. A cup of oil two cups of semolina three of sugar four of water.

Eight hundred euros. Nine hundred at most.

She multiplies the amounts by three – three six nine twelve – and gets to work. She puts the sugar and the water on to boil with two spoonfuls of honey and some orange peel. She pours the oil in another pot with the semolina and cooks it over a low flame stirring constantly, so the semolina will brown slowly and not burn and she'd have to start all over. As soon as the semolina is the proper color, she takes the orange peel out of the other pot and pours the syrup over the semolina which hisses and spits and it surprises Ellie who stirs even more quickly now, quick strong movements until the semolina absorbs the syrup and the halva starts to stick together and peel away from the pot.

She takes the pot off the flame, tosses in the almonds, stirs the mixture well, then takes a break to smoke a cigarette.

The lettuce in the basin is dry. The heart of the lettuce looks white in the dim light. Small and tender and white. Ellie reaches out and gently touches the heart of the lettuce and strokes it gently.

Outside it's getting dark. Black birds sit rustling their wings on the electrical wires like notes on the staff of some strange music, some music written to be played on the last night of the world.

· · ·

She pats down the halva and smooths the golden surface with the wooden spatula and lights another cigarette. The smell of halva spreads through the house and for a moment disguises the smell of Friday and the smell of loneliness and the smell of the malicious poverty slowly and silently and confidently gnawing at Ellie's dreams and strength and life – and those of anyone who lives to work, who is born and lives and dies for work. For a handful of bills.

Malicious vulgar poverty. It too has become a creature of the house. A creature of the house, a pet rat.

. . .

She spreads her best tablecloth on the kitchen table and empties the halva directly on top of it. She starts kneading it and shaping it with slow careful motions until it starts to look like a person. With her hands she forms the legs and neck and head. She uses a fingernail to carve the eyes and nose and a big smiling mouth. The hair should be long and loose, but she has less luck there. She lets it go, though, since she doesn't want to start over.

It doesn't matter, Ellie says. Too much hair would be hard to digest.

When she finishes she lifts the tablecloth carefully by the corners and carries it into the bedroom and lays it out on the bed. She tosses the covers onto the floor and brings the bottle of wine in from the kitchen along with her glass and cigarettes.

She sits on the bed with her knees up and settles in and pulls the tablecloth close.

All for a handful of money, Ellie says. Eight or nine hundred at most.

I don't get it, says Ellie. If poor people do things like that to other poor people what on earth are rich people supposed to do to us.

Christ, I just don't get it.

I'm Ellie Drakou.

I don't understand.

Outside the rain has stopped but drops of water are still dripping from the balcony railing. Look at that, Ellie says, how strange, tonight even the metal bars are crying.

Then she takes a little silver spoon from the pocket of her old lilac bathrobe and sits up straighter on the bed and wraps the bathrobe tighter and starts to eat the semolina man – chewing slowly in the dark and listening to the darkness growing outside as with sharp tiny bites she slowly eats this most recent of men to have passed through her life through her unguarded borders like a conquering soldier or a hunted migrant.

The Tin Soldier

THEY CAUGHT HIM again today, the fucking idiot, and messed him up real bad. Security guys with ponytails and earrings – two of them held him down while four more pummeled him. By the shipyards in Perama. The workers were having some protest because two guys got killed on a fuel boat so he went down and started shouting slogans and spray-painting shit all over the walls. Who knows what he was shouting and writing. What he thought he was doing down there with the jackhammers and sandblasters. Fucking idiot. I could understand if he were some party hardliner – they stick together and look out for their own, they know the tricks. But no, our little fool marches himself down to every rally and demonstration in town, and I have to run around afterward to hospitals and cops to pick up the pieces. He ditched his job, too, and hasn't set foot at home in a month. What does he eat, where does he sleep? What does he do for money? Fucking fucking idiot. He's given us all heart attacks. The bum. The stupid fool.

You stupid jackass, I say to him over the phone. It's the same shit every time. You never learn. Who do you think you are, you spoiled ass.

Oh brave soldier, he says to me. Oh brave soldier, who can save you from death?

Hans Christian Andersen, he says.

The tin soldier.

Remember?

. . .

So here I am racing down to Perama in the middle of the night to get him out even though last time I swore that was it. I put in a call to the commanding officer and told him who I was. Come and get him, he said, and tell him if he keeps it up he's going to get what's coming to him. I told the officer he'd been beaten pretty badly and taken to the hospital. It wasn't any of ours, sir, he said, those guys are always beating on each other, anarchists commies we can't keep them straight. What can you say to an asshole like that. I kept my mouth shut, just thank you truly indebted, and then we both hung up.

Kokkinia Keratsini Amfiali I drive with the doors locked and the windows rolled up. I was born and raised in this part of town but when I left I never looked back – even now I'm passing through as fast as I can with my eyes trained on the road – born and raised here but I don't want to remember, things from the past are old wounds and if you scratch them they start bleeding and get infected and stink. Petros Rallis Street Laodiceia Salamina foot on the gas I run a red light with memories standing like Odysseus's sirens, one on each corner, winking at me at every light, singing for me to stop. A kiss, a cigarette in the rain, a friend you hugged one drunk late night. My father. He may have worked all his life in Perama on those crummy boats but he knew a thing or two about memories. Memories are like ingrown toenails, he used to say when we were kids. Pain death love everything in life is an ingrown toenail. You can trim them but you can't pull them out. Not if you want to survive.

My father. Dead at fifty-two from fumes in the hold. My father. Another memory, a nail that grew backwards into the flesh until it was deep and black.

. . .

Kokkinia Keratsini Amfiali foot on the gas because I had another bad dream and knew I'd be running around again and the anxiety's been eating me up. I dreamed that the two of us were in this place separated by a huge pane of glass and he was standing behind the glass and talking to me but I couldn't hear what he was saying and he pressed his hands to the pane and was trying to tell me something but I couldn't hear. I could only see him shouting, could see the smudges from his hands on the glass and I tried to find some gap somewhere where I could get

25

across but I couldn't find anything. Then he pulled out a can of spray paint and started to write on the glass but I couldn't read the letters and I shouted that I couldn't read what he was writing but he couldn't hear me either so he kept covering the glass with black letters that I couldn't read and afterward we looked at one another through the glass and he stopped writing stopped speaking and just stared at me hands at his sides eyes dripping with a sorrow I can't even describe and then I took off my shirt and wrapped it around my hand and started to pound on the glass to break it but it was like pounding a wall and then I saw my shirt turning red and I started to shout – and that's how I woke up, shouting with my hands clenched into fists pounding the mattress and I started and nearly fell out of bed onto the floor.

Who knows what he was shouting and writing.

That kid is a heart attack. In real life and in my sleep, too.

. . .

Kokkinia Keratsini Amfiali foot full to the floor eyes on the road, and off near Salamina it must be raining, lightning keeps flashing in the sky like uprooted trees and I think how they must have messed him up real bad this time, for him to go on about Hans Christian Anderson and the tin soldier, I'm sure they've split him wide open and probably bashed his head, too, and I start shaking like you wouldn't believe my foot quaking on the gas and the car jumps forward in little leaps like it's got the hiccups and I think about pulling over onto the shoulder for a minute to try and calm down but I know I'm already late and I'm afraid of what might happen if it gets any later. And then at a stoplight out the corner of my eye I see a lame dog hopping along on the sidewalk and I remember. I remember the day we buried our father, how when we got home he made our mother and me sit on the couch and then put an arm around each of us and said that if dogs can learn to live with only three legs then we'd learn to live with just us three – a kid eleven or twelve years old, a little half-pint, where did he learn to talk like that – and if my mother's kisses that night had been tears they would have drowned the whole earth, but in the end he was right. In the end we learned to live like a three-legged dog and ever since my mother has always said – take care, she says to me, take care take care take care you poor thing.

Take care of that boy. A dog can live with three legs but not with two.

Take care.

. . .

He's waiting for me outside the station. From a distance I know it's him but from close up he's unrecognizable. His head like an old soldier's boot, scratched and lumpy and bruised. His forehead is bandaged and his lips are swollen and the sleeve of his shirt is torn all the way up his arm. He gets into the car and sits there quietly, doesn't say anything doesn't look at me. I stare at his swollen lips and remember. All I'm good for these days is remembering. I remember years ago when I took him to the dentist and he came out after his appointment and his lips were swollen just like now and I said what happened were you and she kissing the whole time and he couldn't speak but he smiled and I felt a sorrow and bitterness so strong at the sight of him smiling with those swollen lips and tonight I feel that same sorrow and bitterness seeing him wrapped in bandages with his clothes all torn and I say to myself if I had any guts I'd blow it all sky high – the station the shipyards all of Perama and then Nikaia and Amfiali too, I'd wipe them off the map forever.

I hand him a cigarette – they took his, he says, looking for dope – and we sit in the car and smoke with the windows cracked and it starts to rain and we watch the rain making little rivulets on the windshield and –

Last time, I tell him. It's done, game over. You hear? Last time.

Okay, he says. I hear you. Okay.

His voice comes out deep and muffled as if he's got rags stuffed in his mouth. He rolls down the window and tosses out his cigarette butt and watches the lightning over by Salamina flashing in the sky like uprooted trees. He hasn't shaven and smells of sweat and his hair is like a thick tangled wig. Look at that, I say to myself. The third leg of the dog. Except families don't have legs. They're not dogs. I don't know what they are. Maybe snakes. But not dogs, that's for sure.

He looks at his shredded sleeve and tries to roll it into some kind of shape then sees it isn't working and gives up.

Let's get out of here, he says. Let's go. I want to show you something.

I turn the key in the ignition and start driving. The windshield wipers are on high but they don't stand a chance against this rain, the glass is one big torrent of rain gushing down. We turn onto the avenue and I pull into the right-hand lane and we drive over a pothole full of black water and I curse the hour and the day – take care, my mother says, take care take care of the boy a dog can't live with only two legs – and suddenly I realize I have no idea where we're going, there's no place in this world for the two of us to go and that shaking comes over me again and I don't know what to do.

Pull over, I hear him say. Here. A little further. Here.

I stop. My foot is trembling on the brake. He rolls down the window and points.

Look, he says. I made that. Look. What do you think?

On a high wall there's a painting of an old-style soldier in blue pants and a red coat all buttoned up. He's missing a leg. He has on a yellow belt, a tall black hat and he's holding a black rifle against his shoulder.

He gets out of the car and goes and stands in front of the wall, looks up at the soldier and points. He's already drenched, the bandage is loose and hanging from his forehead like a flap of skin.

Okay, Picasso, I shout. It's great. Now get in the car. We're leaving.

The tin soldier, he says. Remember how he used to tell us that story when we were kids? It was the only fairytale he knew, and he raised us on it. Remember? Remember how sad his voice used to get? Oh brave soldier, who can save you from death. Remember how his voice used to break at the part about the ballerina standing on one leg? And the soldier thought she was missing a leg just like him and he fell in love with her. That tin soldier loved the ballerina so much. It was terrible. To want something so badly and not be able to have it. Remember? Remember the part where the tin soldier finds the ballerina again and feels like crying tin tears but stops himself because he's a soldier and soldiers don't cry? And that's how he stayed until the very end. Solid and strong and silent looking straight ahead with his gun on his shoulder. Until the end. Until a fire melted him down, everything but his little tin heart. Until then he stayed solid and strong with his gun on his shoulder. Until then. Remember? Remember?

He's drenched, dripping all over as if every pore in his skin is an eye and every eye is crying. It's raining harder. Raining with hatred, like a punishment. Lightning keeps flashing across the sky. It's like there's a war on up there – light warring with darkness. A war. Light battling to enter the world and someone battling to shut it out, to seal up all the cracks, to sink the world in darkness.

My foot a jackhammer on the brake.

Get inside, man, I shout. I'm leaving. Get in.

He stares at me and his lips form a swollen smile and then he puts his arms at his sides and lifts his left leg and hops to find his balance then stands stock still with his arms glued to his sides stock still staring far off into the darkness.

In a thousand years, I hear him say. In a thousand years if the world still exists maybe the things that are happening now will have become fairytales. And parents will tell their children stories about strange people who once lived and died for a handful of cash and the children will listen with their mouths hanging open and all these things will seem magical and unreal. In a thousand years. Who knows. Maybe the workers and the poor people of today will be the tin soldiers of the next millennium. Or the dragons and witches. If the world still exists. And if people still tell fairytales. Who knows.

Get in the car, I shout – and I pound hard on the horn so it drowns out the thunder and I rev the engine with my foot which is quaking as if it's not my foot but some stranger's. Come on, I shout. Get inside. Get in.

But he's standing there stock still on one leg in front of the one-legged soldier on the wall, looking off into the darkness with his eyes wide open staring into the darkness with the rain pouring down, heavy gray rain like tin, raindrops falling on him like bullets from the war taking place in the sky, the war between darkness and light – and he stands there stock still staring at the dark with his eyes wide open.

My brother a tin soldier.

Unmoving, unspeaking, unarmed.

Magical and unreal, a creature for the fairytales of the next millennium.

Mao

Everyone calls him Mao. Because the rumor is when he was born he was as yellow as a little Chinese baby. Even his mother and his sisters call him Mao. His father was killed in a gas explosion in Perama years ago. A communist but an easygoing friendly guy. He's the one who gave him that name. Mao. And even now that he's a tall strong young man everyone in the neighborhood still calls him that.

What's up, Mao?

Fuck you all.

His older sister Katerina got raped last summer behind the Katrakeio Theater where the quarries used to be. Apparently it was these ten or so guys from around Memou Square in Korydallos. We never saw her again after that. Her mother sent her to live with relatives on some island – Chios or maybe Samos. No one knows for sure, they're keeping it a secret. Katerina was a pretty girl, the whole neighborhood always said so. Tall and thin with yellow hair and grey eyes. A tender thing. Everywhere she went people always turned to look. But from a young age she got mixed up with a bad crowd and late nights and that kind of story never ends well. Everyone always told her mother keep an eye on that girl keep an eye on Katerina but what could she do a woman raising three kids on her own. Who goes around all day selling tupperware and pots and pans from house to house to try and make ends meet. The younger daughter Thomai is exactly the opposite. She's a pretty girl too but she took after her father. From home to school and school to home and never any surprises. She doesn't care about friends and cafés. She's a top student and speaks foreign languages and even plays the accordion. Her father was crazy about the accordion but he never got a chance to hear her play – she hadn't even been baptized when he was killed in that explosion in Perama. They named her after him. His name was Thomas so they named her Thomai. And in the evenings when we hear her practicing her accordion the whole neighborhood remembers him. A dyed-in-the-wool communist but a quiet man – he wouldn't have hurt an ant.

The September after they kicked Katerina out of the house Mao dropped out of high school and got a job at a billiards parlor up in Perivolaki. His mother still hasn't forgiven him for it. She can't stomach the idea of her son putting an apron on every day and carrying coffees and sandwiches and beers to the customers. They fight about it all the time. Though really it's just the widow who does the fighting – Mao never says a thing.

Not a single word. It's terrifying. And then he goes outside and sits on the steps all night and smokes and talks to the stray dogs and cats. And everyone in the neighborhood sees him and none of us knows what to say.

Mao's changed a lot since last year. Not that he ever had much give and take with anyone but now you can't even get a full sentence out of him. Michalis Panigirakis whose father used to work in the graveyard and who knows about these things says Mao has the look of death in his eyes. He says Mao knows who hurt his sister and he's saving up to buy a gun and hunt them down. He says Mao found some guys from Mani who can get him a good handgun for a thousand or so. Michalis says the guys from Korydallos sent Mao a message that if he dares make a move they'll break into his house at night and tear his mother and little sister to shreds. And they'll pin Mao down in the corner and make him watch.

That's why Mao doesn't sleep at night. He keeps watch outside the house in case the guys from Korydallos come around.

True or false that's what Michalis says. But what precisely is going on in Mao's head no one could say for sure. Because Mao doesn't tell anyone anything. He doesn't talk to anyone but the cats.

That whole business has been going on for a while. He's got all the cats and dogs in the neighborhood coming around since he feeds them and pets them and talks to them. On Sundays he throws crumbs on the sidewalk for the pigeons and doves and sparrows. He's got a cat with one bum leg that he calls Augustus. It's a female not a male but that's what he calls it, Augustus. He picked her out from the crowd and put a red string around her neck with a little bell. And his mother sees it all happening and it drives her nuts. Everyone agrees that something needs to be done because every day there's some kind of ruckus in the neighborhood with all those dogs and cats but who would dare say anything to Mao about it. Because he was always kind of a loner but now he looks at you and your blood freezes. The other day he shaved his head and since he's just skin and bones when he stares at you with those grim black eyes he looks just like one of those kids who starved to death during the occupation.

No one even dares call him Mao to his face anymore.

What's up, Mao?

Fuck you all.

. . .

At night Mao doesn't sleep. He sits on the steps outside the house and drinks and smokes and talks to Augustus the cat. It's a great comfort in the middle of the night to hear his voice and the tinkling of the cat's bell. A great comfort. Every so often he gets up and walks back and forth like a watchman. Down to Ikoniou Street and then back again to Kastamoni and Tzavelas. Back and forth all night every night. On October nights when it rains and all you can hear is the water running through the drain pipes and emptying into the grates on street corners. On December nights when the wind whistles through the electrical wires and the branches of the mulberry tree scratch the window like hands frozen with cold. In March when the nights are cool and you stick your head out the window and inhale the scent of the bitter orange trees and look up at the stars in the sky and the scattered clouds and wonder if something might happen after all – if something might happen so the world doesn't vanish and all the people with it. Mao is there. All night every night. Until daybreak. No one knows how he can go to work on so little sleep.

It's a great comfort. It's a great comfort to know that some-one is awake out there in the street. And if you open your eyes and your ears you'll see and hear things you never notice during the day, in the yellow light of day. As if objects change with the hours. As if night has some secret plan, some magical power that can alter things and make them seem less wild less harsh – can offer some drop of comfort to the heart of a fright-ened person. As if god hasn't abandoned the world entirely but decided to exist only at night. If you open your eyes and ears you'll see and hear. The sudden swipe of the hand, the *tsaf*, the flame from the match lighting the cigarette. The smoke rising yellow from Mao's mouth and scattering like frozen breath in the darkness. The tip of the cigarette glowing on and off like a firefly. The cat stretching on Mao's lap so his fingers can get at all the best places. You'll hear the tinkling of the bell and Mao's voice murmuring who knows what. You'll hear the sound of his bottle coming to rest on the steps beside him. The thud of his heels as he paces up and down the street.

A comfort. It's a great comfort to know someone in the neighborhood is staying up at night. Of course the whole neighborhood feels sorry for Mao but at the same time since things happened the way they did it's good that we have someone watching over us at night – even if that isn't his purpose. There are about a hundred families living around here. And things have gotten pretty rough. Drugs in the school. Purse snatchers. Thieves. Down near Agios Nikolas three houses got broken into in a single week. One guy and his wife went to pick their kid up from school and when they got home there were three guys with knives in the house, there in broad daylight. Even the Pakistanis are out of control. The Pakistanis. Who never even used to meet your eye. Now they roam through the streets at night like gangs. The other day they grabbed a kid off his bike and took him down to the field by the church of Osia Xeni and hurt him bad. A little kid just ten years old.

Things have gotten pretty rough recently.

But we're okay.

Around here we're calmer at night.

Because we've got Mao.

. . .

In the evening the sky darkens and at around nine a quiet rain starts to fall that seeps all the way down to your bones. Just now we heard on the television about what happened last night on Kondyli Street. Two thugs went into a corner store and knifed a girl working there who was seven months pregnant. Kondyli is just a stone's throw from here but we heard it first from the television. And it got us all worked up again. The admiral blames the police for everything. Vayios who works in construction driving a backhoe and has a cop for a brother blames the politicians: the leftists hate the police and gutted the force as soon as they could and the guys on the right sat and watched because they're afraid of the left. Michalis says if we had a drop of dignity, if we were real men and not just useless bystanders we'd do what Mao does instead of sitting in front of the television and crying over our fate.

That's what men do, says Michalis. Take the situation into their own hands. We're just chickenshit.

He gets up and turns off the television and lights some candles and brings a bottle of tsipouro and some dried chick peas and raisins. We sit in the dark and look out the window. No matter how bad the fear and rage get you can't help but give yourself over for a while to the sweetness of the rain. You listen to the tap tap tap of the raindrops on the windowsill and they seem to be dripping straight into your heart. And for a little while you forget your troubles. You forget what happened on Kondyli Street and forget that this is the first time it's rained since October and who knows when it will rain again. You listen to the rain and let yourself forget. And if you crack the window open and put your head out and take a deep breath you can smell the wet earth and the scent of the bitter orange trees and the breeze that has a strange acrid smell to it again tonight. And if you look up you'll see the rain falling yellow around the streetlight and if you look even higher you'll see the clouds which have turned a dark yellow as if they've traveled over some burning land to get here.

It's after eleven when Mao comes out of the building sits on the steps and sets his bottle and cigarettes down beside him. It's tsikoudia says Michalis who's seen Mao coming out of the Cretan's shop lots of times over on Tsaldaris Street. Then Mao grabs the cat who's sunk her claws into his shoulder and holds her in his arms and starts to pet her. He looks at the road glistening with rainwater and every so often looks up at the falling rain and the raindrops that are as yellow as an old man's nicotine-drenched beard. And Vayios who's lived here the longest tells us yet again how Mao's grandfather Stavros the ship's captain had a thing for cats too. One day someone brought him a fluffy white cat named Nabila but he was pretty old by then maybe eighty and his hearing wasn't great and he called it Mantila. He was crazy about that cat, never let it out of his sight. One day a few years before he died that cat disappeared. So he goes out into the street in his pajamas with his cane and starts calling Mantila Mantila Mantila. And a neighbor hears him and thinks well the old man must have lost it or had a stroke or something, and she grabs a kitchen towel and goes down into the street and says, here you go barba-Stavros I brought you a kerchief. Now let's go back inside so you don't get hit by a truck or who knows what. And the old man is all upset because he thinks she's making fun of him so he raises his cane and almost finishes the poor woman off. Beats her like you wouldn't believe. They had a heck of a time calming him down, he had one foot in the grave but his blood still boiled. The old bugger. Vicious to the last. The older generation said he'd killed plenty of people during the civil war.

The kid will end up just like his grandfather, Vayios says. Mark my words, Vayios is never wrong. That's how all commies are. Assholes every one.

Commie or not he's a better man than us, says Michalis. You know there are people who won't go to bed until they see Mao come and sit out on those steps? There are people who stay up every night until they see him coming outside. I've heard with my own ears plenty of folk say that they sleep easier at night since Mao started keeping watch. Not just one or two. Lots.

The admiral gets up and goes over to the window. He's a

retired navy man, that's why we call him the admiral. Even his wife calls him that. Sometimes when we're out late at Satanas's place she calls on the phone and doesn't ask for Dimitris or even Pavlakos. She asks for the admiral. Is the admiral there? she says.

He wipes the windowpane with his hand and looks out. He's gotten so thin lately, his clothes are swimming on him. And now in the half-dark his face is as yellow as the leaves on the mulberry tree in winter. The other day he told Vayios that ever since he had to retire he doesn't even recognize himself. He's withered away. It's not right for them to retire men so young, he said. Vayios swore. The rest of us are being ground down by our fucking jobs, you jerk, and you've got it tough just sitting around, huh? Get lost, you good-for-nothing. You spoiled asshole. Things got pretty ugly between the two of them that day.

Just think about it a minute, Michalis says. We're about a hundred families around here, right? Some aren't on speaking terms and others wouldn't even recognize one another in the street. Even in this building there are people I only see on Christmas and Easter. And yet each night we're all on tenterhooks to see whether Mao will go out onto those steps or not. Just the other afternoon my mother had her incense out and was going through the house waving it around and at some point I see her going onto the balcony and waving that thing down toward the street. What are you blessing out there mom

42

I ask. The cats? No she says it's for Mao. So god will be good to that young man who protects us at night. You see what I mean? And just think, she hasn't spoken to Mao's mother in years. But it's a comfort to know that someone is sitting up while you're sleeping. A great comfort. It's a big thing to be able to sleep easily at night. And I'll tell you something else. If there were a Mao in every neighborhood in this city we'd all be better off. Don't laugh. If there were a Mao in every neighborhood keeping watch at night the world would be a better place. I'd bet on it. Don't laugh. That's what real democracy is. When poor people don't wait for the rich to come and save them but take the situation into their own hands. Because that's how the trouble starts: with us thinking that the rich will ever help the poor. It just doesn't happen. We live in two separate worlds. They're over there and we're over here. We have to take the situation into our own hands. And that's exactly what Mao's doing. What do you think man's greatest enemy is? Death? Money? Not at all. It's fear. That's our worst enemy. Fear. Fear.

Something's happening, says the admiral. It's that Mirafiori again. Something's up.

We crowd in front of the window to watch. The yellow Mirafiori is coming down the street with its headlights off and its exhaust pipe growling. The cat lying in Mao's arms lifts her head. When it gets close to Mao the car slows down. Mao stands up and the driver steps on the gas and skids away. Mao runs out into the middle of the road and looks at the car which is all the way down turning left onto Cyprus Street. Then he sits back down. He waits. He looks around. He leans forward and seems to be whispering something into the cat's ear and the cat is listening with her tail up in the air and slightly bent like a question mark. Then Mao takes a swig from the bottle and lights a cigarette and when he exhales the smoke rises out from inside of him thick and yellow as if he'd smoked the whole cigarette in one go.

That's the second time tonight, says Michalis. They came by earlier, too.

How many were in the car? I saw two.

Three. There was another in the back seat.

Things are going to get messy for us with those guys, Vayios says as he walks away from the window. Mark my words. Vayios is never wrong.

. . .

The rain has stopped but raindrops are still trickling down the windowpane and through the half-open window you can hear water running in the street next to the sidewalk like a little stream. The admiral searches for music on the radio and finds some old rembetika but a few minutes later we hear the jingle for the communist station and Vayios says get lost you faggots and goes over and turns the dial.

What's happening?

Nothing.

What's he doing?

Nothing. Playing with the cat.

What's her name again? Julius?

Augustus.

Yeah, that's it. Guys, I told you but you didn't listen. The kid's going to end up just like his shithead grandfather. If he lives that long. Which I doubt. I figure he's gotten mixed up in drugs. All that about his sister and the guys from Korydallos, I'd take it with a grain of salt. Michalis can say what he wants. Did you ever meet a commie you could make any sense of?

I don't know about you, but I remember seventy-eight like it was yesterday, Michalis says. The first time Logothetis was elected mayor, our first commie mayor, not too long after the junta fell. You remember what happened that night? All the guys from the party gathered outside the church of Osia Xeni and shouted as if there was a war on. I was still in grade school but I remember like it was happening now. I remember our mothers coming out into the street and calling us home and locking us up in our houses and all the neighbors being scared shitless. It's all over the commies are going to kill us tonight. They'll break into our houses and slaughter us all. That night we cried until the tears ran dry. You wouldn't believe how terrified we were. The women cried the kids cried the old ladies had fallen on all fours and were crossing themselves and repenting. Total panic, man. And I remember my father rest his soul and two or three others took kitchen knives and kept watch all night at the door to the building. Panic. And we're talking about seventy-eight, right? Not the fifties or even sixties. This was seventy-eight.

That's how it goes, Vayios says. The commies were out of control back then. They thought they were going to turn Kokkinia into another Stalingrad. Now those pests are in Parliament and we pay their salaries on top of it all. It makes me sick. Screw your democracy you fucking frauds. Man, it really makes me sick, those faggots. It makes me sick just looking at them. Especially the ones who sold out and got into the game. Who go around in ties and fancy cars and sit in front of the TV at night with one hand on the remote and the other on their dick dreaming of the revolution. I've got the biggest beef with those assholes. Lefties, sure, you know what that means. There's only one lefty thing on their body, and that's their left nut. The assholes.

The admiral reaches over grabs the bottle and fills the glasses. His hands are shaking. He drinks his down in one swallow and refills his glass and drains it again.

That's nothing, he says. In seventy-one with the political situation they sent us over to Norfolk in America to pick up the Nafkratousa. It was a huge ship the biggest in the fleet.

46

You could fit a whole city on that thing. We stayed over there for about two months and it wasn't easy. Every time we went out things got crazy. I still remember how those black guys went after us. They threw trash down on us from apartment buildings. The war in Vietnam was going strong and when they saw us in uniform they lost it. As if we were to blame for all the slaughter going on over there. We poor fools couldn't have pointed to Vietnam on a map. One night I remember we ran into a navy guy at a bar an American marine who'd just come back from Vietnam and I remember his hands were wrapped in gauze. We started talking and he told us that one night his unit walked straight into a booby trap and everyone was killed except for him and one or two others. And ever since then he couldn't get over it he kept chewing his nails all the way down to the flesh. Out of fear, see. That's why they'd put that gauze on him. And he wasn't some puny thing, he was a big strong guy two meters tall. I still remember him. We bought him beer and whiskey and he wouldn't let us leave. He begged us to sneak him onto the ship and take him with us to Greece. Can you believe it, a man two meters tall acting like a little kid. I still remember him. Anyway. It's all just stories now. But ever since I was a kid I had a thing for America. I always said I would find some way to go and live there forever. And my father rest in peace who'd traveled all over in the navy used to say America isn't for the likes of us. In Europe people think being poor is a matter of bad luck. In America poverty is shameful. Can you bear to be poor and have to feel ashamed of it too? So just sit tight and don't dream those kinds of dreams.

Vayios looks at Michalis and then at the admiral.

Man, where does that fit in? he asks. How did we get from old barba-Stavros's cat to Vietnam? You lost me.

It's something else I'm getting at, says the admiral. In hindsight sitting here thinking it all over I realize my father sold me a bill of goods. I sure didn't get very far here, either. Aren't I poor and ashamed here, too? Thirty-five years on the job and where did I end up? With a family of four living in a tiny hole of an apartment. It took me two years going from politician to politician to find my son a job and now they say they're already going to let him go. He broke his back carrying spare parts for eight hundred euros a month and now they want to fire him because Mrs. Toyota isn't doing too well this year. Instead of five hundred million she only made four hundred and ninety. A real blow for the company, you know? So now here I am running around again begging every slimebag I know to find my son another job. You remember me telling you how that guy Panayiotakos found him the job at the spare parts place? We were together in the navy, he was my first mate on the Panther. If you gave him a ship the incompetent fool would run it into the rocks and now there he is in parliament. Anyway. When he

48

found work for the kid I went to his office down by the public theater to thank him. He happened to be wearing a real strong cologne and when we shook hands the smell stayed on my mine. And guys you won't believe it. It's been how many years since then and every so often I still catch a whiff of that scent on my hand. I mean for god's sake. There are times when I can smell my hand and it makes me want to vomit. Like my soul stinks something awful. Right now for instance. Right now I can smell it.

He brings his hand up to his nose and sniffs it then stretches it out towards Michalis.

See for yourself. See how it smells. How the hell does that happen, can you tell me?

Enough already, says Vayios. Sitting there crying over your lot. Cologne and bullshit. How much was your bonus when you retired? And how much are your checks every month? Do us a favor, man. You're one to talk, retired at fifty and now you sit around scratching your balls and getting paid for it too. Let's change the subject because otherwise things are going to get ugly. Michalis, we kicked this bottle. Are you going to bring another or should I leave?

Michalis brings some more tsipouro fills the glasses and sits back down. Vayios leans over and lights his cigarette from a candle and exhales out the corner of his mouth. He takes the cellophane off the pack and crumples it and tosses it into the ashtray glancing sideways at Pavlakos who's turned his head and is staring out the window.

On the subject of money, says Michalis. Last year when my father died Iraklis came by here one night. You know Iraklis, who lives on the corner. Lakis.

The guy with the beard, you mean. Who has a stall at the market.

That guy. He came pretty late after you guys had left. So he comes over with a flask of whisky and we sit in the bedroom because the women were in here mourning with my mother. So we're drinking pretty hard and at some point the guy starts crying and talking to me about my father and what a good person he was and how much he loved him and how my father was like a brother to him and stuff like that. And there he is crying and hugging me and I don't know what to do. At some point he turns to me and asks how much the funeral is going to cost. And I tell him. And he says, listen Michalis since your father was like a brother to me and you guys here aren't doing so well I want to pay for the funeral. I'll give you the money. So my soul will be clean as they say. I'll give you the money. I can see the guy's blind drunk with tears streaming down his face so I say come on Lakis what's all this? I mean thanks and all but that's not how things work. You think I'd let you pay for my own father's funeral? I couldn't do that. To make a long story short the guy won't take no for an answer. And

I say to myself this asshole is pulling my chain because I know him well and I know he's a dirty jew as cheap as they come. But guys, he actually gets up and says wait I'll be back and in ten minutes he's back with an envelope full of hundred-euro bills. I'm telling you, it was bursting with hundreds. And he calls my mother in and tells her too and the poor woman is so dazed she starts shouting and crying and bending down to kiss his hands. She actually kissed his hands. Because we'd been doing the rounds asking for loans from cousins and uncles. To make a long story short the next morning I go over to that cheat Kioseoglou and pull out the cash for the coffin and the flowers and all the rest. Then around noon or so Iraklis calls me up and tells me what happened. Listen man, he says, I messed up, that money was my wife's who had it to pay some bills and the kids' schools and shit like that. And he keeps crying and saying he's sorry over and over. And I was frozen there with the receiver in my hand. I almost fainted.

So what did you do? the admiral asks. Did you give it back?

Of course. What else could I do. I ran around to all my relatives and came up with the money and gave it back to him. And just think, the coward didn't even come and get it himself. He sent his daughter. The coward.

Are you kidding? says Vayios. That much of a fag? And you never said anything to us all this time?

Say what? Like it would change anything? It just came up

now in conversation. For a while I didn't even tell my mother. And the poor woman came to me after the funeral and asked me where Iraklis was and why he hadn't been there and she sang that scumbag's praises. Nothing like that had ever happened to me before. When he handed me that envelope I swear to god it was like a weight dropped from my shoulders. I was in pretty bad shape but I said to myself look at that, god finally took pity on us for once. And then that shame. A shame like you wouldn't believe. Me running around an hour before the funeral begging for five hundred euros from one guy and five hundred from another. I was so ashamed. I wanted the earth to open up and swallow me whole. The worst shame of my life. Then again what comes around goes around. I'm sure you've heard what happened with his son.

Whose? Vayios asks.

What do you mean whose? Are you drunk already? Who've we been talking about this whole time? Didn't you hear what happened to his son? They sent him to Rhodes to study and he came back an end-stage junkie. The other day he had a fit and grabbed his mother by the neck and almost strangled her. And now they've locked him up in a clinic down in Voula or Glyfada and are paying out the nose. That's how it works, man. What goes around comes around. Ever since the day of the funeral I've been praying for something to happen to make that bastard pay for what he did to me. When I found out about his son I was so happy. It's strange. How strong hatred can be. Sometimes I think hatred is like the air we breathe in this city. It may be killing you slowly but you still can't live without it.

Michalis takes off his glasses and examines them in the light of the candle then puts them back on. The admiral is shriveled in his chair with his head bowed staring at his shoes. Vayios gets up and goes over to the window. He bends down and looks outside. The glass steams up from his breath.

I sure see you guys together a lot, he says. Weren't you sitting with him the other day at Satanas's?

I know, says Michalis. No one else will talk to him and he always comes over to me. He's pathetic. Drunk all day long. What is it, admiral? Why the long face? Did I offend you?

The admiral lights a cigarette, blows the smoke straight over the flame which quivers for a moment then rights itself again.

No, Michalis, he says. I'm not offended. It's something else I'm thinking about. We talk and talk and the more we talk the better I understand that what binds us together are the things we're afraid of and the things we hate. How did we end up like this? Where did all the hatred and fear come from, can you tell me? And the more time passes the worse things get. Some days I see things that make me want to kill someone. My lord. I went through hell on the ships all those years but I never felt a thing like that. Never. But now it's too much. I'm drowning, you know? Drowning.

Michalis looks at Vayios who's still standing at the window and Vayios winks without smiling and puts a finger to his lips then taps that same finger on the side of his head. He comes back from the window and sits down across from the admiral and fills all the glasses again. He drinks, then bends down to light another cigarette from the candle.

It's bad luck, says the admiral.

Vayios stays there bent over the candle staring at him holding the cigarette between his teeth. In the half-dark his face fills with strange frightening shadows.

It's bad luck to light your cigarette from a candle. On the ships we used to say that if you light your cigarette from a candle a sailor will die.

What do you care, Michalis said. You're on dry land now.

The admiral lifts his head and looks at us like a man coming out of a coma trying to figure out who all the people are standing around him. His eyes are foggy like two steamed-up windows.

Then he leans over and blows in the direction of the candle. The flame bends to the side and nearly goes out but then springs upright again.

. . .

One weekend last month Mao came out onto the steps later than usual. It had been raining all day and when night came a thick fog fell all around and if you looked carefully you could see steam rising from the wet asphalt like frozen breath – as if there were something alive in there, some strange creature with a thousand mouths breathing in the dark. As soon as he got outside he made a *psspss* sound and the cat jumped out from behind a pile of cardboard boxes stacked outside of Yiota's corner store and limped over to him at a run. Mao folded up one of the boxes and put it down on the steps and sat down and set his cigarettes and his bottle of booze next to him then grabbed the cat by the neck as she rubbed up against his legs with her tail in the air and lifted her into his lap and started petting and talking to her. And the night was so peaceful that if you listened hard you could hear the raindrops still falling from the branches of the mulberry tree and the gurgling of the water running in the street by the sidewalk and you could hear the tinkling of the cat's bell and Mao saying things you wouldn't expect to hear from a kid like him. Wistful things full of nostalgia. A young kid like that – what on earth did he have to feel nostalgic about? And his voice was so sweet and calm, even calmer than the night, a murmur like the gurgling of the water in the street by the sidewalk. And if you closed your eyes you felt a strange peace spreading inside you until the gurgling of the water and Mao's voice ran together. Because everyone says it's a great comfort to hear a human voice in the night. It's a great comfort to know someone else is kept up by fear – to know someone is doing something to send that fear away.

Only Michalis saw what happened that night.

He was sitting in the living room watching a documentary about what the end of the world will be like and at some point he got pretty alarmed and turned off the television and put on the radio and poured himself a whiskey. His mother was in the bedroom with her girlfriends listening to songs on the television. They have a habit of all gathering at Michalis's house because they're widows and don't like to be alone at night. And Michalis is always chiding his mother and telling her that she's turned the house into an old folks' home but she doesn't pay any attention. When the bottle was empty he went in and woke up the old ladies who were sleeping there with the television on. He took them all home then came back and pulled a blanket over his mother and went into the living room and opened a new bottle and undressed and lit a cigarette and then sat as he did every night beside the window and watched Mao who was sitting on the steps and smoking and drinking and talking to his cat.

Michalis likes sitting in the dark at night and watching Mao. Lots of times it occurs to him to take his bottle of whiskey down and sit next to Mao on the steps and put an arm around him and pat his shaved head and tell the kid to talk to him instead of the cat. There are lots of nights when he's thought of doing that. It wouldn't bother him at all to stay up all night and go straight to work sleepless and still drunk. But he knows Mao doesn't want other people around. And if anyone else in the neighborhood saw him they'd all start whispering behind his back. Better to lose an eye than your reputation – right? Right.

It was after three when the Mirafiori showed up. It came down from Cyprus Street the wrong way on a one-way street and crept along with its lights off until it stopped in front of Mao's house. Michalis saw the brake lights come on and yellow smoke rising from the exhaust pipe. He saw the big yellow scorpion painted on the back window. He stood up and opened the window. He waited. He thought about putting on some clothes because the damp chilled him to the bone – but he didn't have time. Mao jumped to his feet and the cat leapt from his arms with a wild hiss and then Mao hurled himself against the passenger's side door. The Mirafiori sped off, its tires skidding over the wet asphalt. Mao ran after it. Outside the deafmute's house he stopped and threw an arm forward and a gunshot rang out – a dry empty bam like a branch breaking. Then there was the sound of shattering glass. The Mirafiori turned the wrong way onto Kastamoni and disappeared. Michalis was hanging naked from the window. He wanted to shout something down to Mao but no sound came out. He saw Mao standing in the middle of the road with his arm stretched out and his legs spread and bowed like a cowboy's. Michalis expected to see lights coming on and doors opening and people running out of their homes but none of that happened. Mao went to the corner. He looked up and down the street. He looked up at the sky that vanished into the fog. Then he walked back slowly looking straight ahead his boots thudding on the pavement. Tall and so thin – a shadow with no body.

When he got back to the steps he took a swig from his bottle and lit a cigarette. The cat was watching him from where she'd scrambled up into the mulberry tree. He called to her but she didn't come over. A light came on in the house. Mao tossed his cigarette to the ground and started to run.

Michalis hung naked from the window and watched as Mao disappeared at the end of the street. The darkness fell on him like an enormous shadow that had finally found its body.

True or false that's what Michalis said.

· · ·

The next morning we gathered at the deafmute's house. There were at least ten of us there, maybe more. The deafmute was really pissed. The bullet had shattered the windshield of his car. He kept cursing Mao with his hands and Mao's mother and his own bad luck because he always parked his car in front of his house but the night before some stranger had taken his spot so he had to park his car on the corner. He waved his hands and rolled his eyes and the veins in his neck bulged like they might burst. Someone said it was the whole neighborhood's fault since no one called the police and someone else said no one realized the sound was gunfire – who ever heard of such a thing, guns going off in the middle of our street – and then the first guy said we were all chickenshit pussies and if he'd been here last night – he was at a wedding – he would have grabbed the bastard by the throat and shoved the gun up his ass. Pretty soon all hell broke loose since the calmer among us were getting annoyed with the deafmute who kept thrashing around and saying mmmmm nnnnnn and we told him to sit down and shut up so we could figure out what to do and the deafmute got even angrier and turned bright red and grabbed a telephone book and started banging it on the table. Everyone was furious and scared. Some people wanted to go down to the police station and others were cursing Mao's mother who wandered the streets like a priest's dog and had turned her house into a bordello. One guy said that women are the world's great weakness and ever since they started to do other things than the only one they're made for – which is to say having babies and raising them – they'd ruined themselves and their kids and all the men in the world. And everyone said something had to be done because who ever heard of a bratty doped-up bastard out loose in the streets with a gun in his hand and if we don't do something for sure tomorrow or the next day he'll go out and shoot the first guy he sees. And Iraklis with the beard who has a stall in the market asked who wanted to come with him to Mao's house to beat the kid up and someone said Mao never came home last night. Everyone was furious and scared. Then Michalis said let's not go overboard we have to find some way of dealing with the situation. He reminded us that Mao guards the whole neighborhood and lots of people feel safer knowing someone is staying up at night and watching over things. And let's not forget what Mao went through with his sister. Let's not forget that those assholes from Korydallos swore they were going to come to his house one night and hurt his mother and his little sister.

Are you crazy, Michalis? Vayios jumped in. You mean because they fucked his sister it's fine if he fucks us next? Do us a favor and get lost, the last thing we need is you taking his side.

Yeah, Iraklis said. And how do we even know that's how it went down? How do we know what happened? I'm telling you, the asshole's gotten mixed up in drugs and that's why they're after him. It's as clear as day. And I'm sure that little whore was into something too and that's why they kicked her out of the house. And the mother's just covering the whole thing up. What's all this shit about guarding the neighborhood. Guarding my ass. Don't try and turn some junkie into a hero.

Eventually they agreed that Michalis and Iraklis would go together to talk to Mao's mother and see what the hell could be done. The people who initially wanted to go straight to the police agreed because someone said that if the police got involved Mao and the guys from Korydallos might all come after us and then we'd be up shit creek – this is dangerous stuff not fun and games. Better for us to take care of things ourselves without involving the cops.

So that's what happened. Only Mao's mother said she didn't know where Mao was. She said she was out of her mind with worry that he might do something stupid with that gun. She said she didn't know what kind of gun it was or where he'd gotten it. She didn't know anything.

The others want to go to the police, Michalis said. We convinced them not to, but it wasn't easy.

I know, the woman said. They should go. I'll go with them. I don't know what else to do.

Then she said she'd talked to Mao's boss at the Lido who promised to try and track her son down. He told her to wait until afternoon. Don't worry, he said. Leave it to me. I know how to find him.

Fine, Iraklis said when he heard that. But there's the mute, too. You know your boy broke his windshield? What are we going to do about that? Who's going to pay for the damage?

The woman looked at them and then collapsed into a chair and started to sob. She was shaking all over, she couldn't breathe. Her daughter Thomai went over and hugged her and tried to wipe her mother's eyes with the sleeve of her pajamas. Then the woman got up and opened a drawer and pulled out a fifty-euro bill.

What is that? Iraklis said. What are we supposed to do with that, woman? You can't even buy a pair of wipers for fifty euros, much less a new windshield.

It's all I have, she said. I'll get more by the end of the week. This is all I have right now. I don't have anything else.

Okay, said Michalis.

No way, man, Iraklis cut him off. You think he's going to get off with fifty euros? He could have killed someone last night. No way.

It's all I have, the woman repeated. Take it and leave me to my worry. Where's my son? My Mao. Why don't you go out looking for him? What did you do to him? Where's my Mao?

The daughter who'd been watching silently all this time went into her room and came back out carrying her accordion.

Take this, she told Michalis. It's German. It's worth at least a thousand euros. Take it and leave us alone.

The mother looked at the girl and then at the men. She seemed not to understand what was happening. She was bobbing her head up and down like a broken doll. Her blouse had slipped down on one shoulder and you could see her bra strap. It was pink.

Let's go, man, said Michalis and grabbed the other guy by the elbow. Come on, let's go. Move it.

Iraklis reached out a hand and pressed a black button on the accordion. It made no sound at all. The girl shrank from him. Her shoulders trembled and her cheeks were bright red.

We're not through, said Iraklis. Don't think you're going to get off so easy. You can tell your son I'm waiting for him. Tell him that's what Iraklis said. I'm waiting. He won't get off so easy, you hear? I dance a tough dance.

When they went outside they stood on the sidewalk to light cigarettes. It was windy and it took a few tries to get the cigarettes burning properly.

You noticed, right? Asked Iraklis.

What?

Her mouth, man. It stank from a thousand meters. From all those blow jobs. She reminded me of a girl I did once in Keratsini. An incredible whore. Didn't leave a single dick limp. Just like this one here.

He turned around and looked at the house.

But the girl isn't bad. A fresh young thing. You could eat her for dinner.

What are we going to do about the deafmute, Michalis said.

Fuck that crybaby pussy. We'll see what we can do with that

girl, though. Wouldn't say no to a piece of her. Anyway. We'll see. How about an ouzo at Satanas's? My treat.

. . .

Mao's been missing since that Saturday night. No one knows what happened to him. And his mother and sister are lying low too. Michalis went by the house once or twice but no one was home. He says maybe they went to that island where they sent the older girl, Katerina. Or maybe they're staying somewhere else for a while until the whole thing blows over. Who knows.

Meanwhile there have been developments in the neighborhood. Last week they brought some of those big blue bins from the municipality for recycling and put one on each corner and sent around flyers and some special bags for us to collect our papers and cans. Progress. On Thursday night when we were sitting at Satanas's the admiral came and asked if we'd heard what happened to that guy Sofronis who lives next to the school.

What happened, said Vayios. Did he die?

He's lost it, the poor guy, said the admiral. Last night my son was coming home from work and found him trying to climb into the recycling bin. He caught him just in time. What are you doing, barba-Tasos, he says. Are you crazy? You're trying to get into the trash? And the guy turns around and you know what he says? Let me be, Stefanos, he says. Just let me be. A man who lets his wife die like that is fit for the trash. They can pick me up and recycle me and maybe I'll come out a better man. Just listen to that. Listen to the things that happen out there in the world. My son could barely hold him back. And then he sat on the street corner and laughed to himself like a crazy person. Things are not going well around here. I've said it before. Things are not going well.

I remember his wife, said Michalis. She struggled with the hospitals and doctors for a while. Cancer, right, admiral? I'm pretty sure.

The admiral ordered a half kilo of ribs and some tsipouro for the table. He started to say something about Sofronis and his wife but saw that no one was interested. No one spoke. Outside a wind had picked up and we could hear the windowpanes creaking and the wind whistling through the cracks. It was almost eleven. Satanas had turned off the TV and was standing behind the bar watching us.

Tomorrow I'm going to go see my kid at the clinic, Iraklis said. They said we should take him out for the day now that it's the weekend. They say it'll do him good. Keep him from going nuts. But his mother is scared and doesn't want to come. She doesn't want me to go either. She's scared. So I don't know what to do.

How old is he? Asked Vayios.

Twenty. Going on twenty-one.

Take him to a Russian. He doesn't need a family outing. He

needs a woman. That's the only way to keep him from going nuts in the state he's in.

As for my kid, they're going to lay him off at the end of the month, the admiral said. He found out yesterday. But I'd already warned him. Take care, I told him. Take care not to lose your faith. Don't do them the favor and lose your faith. You have to believe. There may be no god but you have to believe. Your belief is god. That's what I told him. But the whole thing's hit him pretty hard. Last night I got up out of bed and found him smoking on the balcony. I didn't know what to do, him leaning over the railing like that. It made my blood run cold. I sat in the dark and watched and I was so scared.

Iraklis put out his cigarette and got up.

I'm going, he said. I have an early morning tomorrow.

As he left his foot caught on a chair and it fell to the floor. He didn't even look back.

The admiral tipped his glass back and emptied it then filled it again. His hands were shaking. He looked out the window at Iraklis who had bent over next to a car trying to light a cigarette out of the wind. He took a sip then bowed his head and shut his eyes and started to speak with his eyes closed.

I still believe, he said. I really do. Recently I've been lying in bed at night making up stories. Like I've discovered some magic potion that makes me invisible and I steal money from the banks and distribute it to everyone. Or that I buy a big estate high up over the sea and build a house that would make you stare. Villa Constantina. That's what I call it. And I build five or six more little houses out of stone and I give one to everyone and we all live there together a happy life. My daughter takes charge of the garden and the trees and the flowers. I make my son the foreman. He's the foreman together with Iraklis's kid and Mao. I give them each a solid wage and a nice car and they're real happy. Mao's mother and older sister are in charge of the kitchen. They go out shopping and decide what to cook stuff like that. And the other sister the younger one plays music for us at night while we're eating and having a good time. Sure. I've thought of everything. Down to the smallest detail. And I've built all kinds of things on the estate. A huge room out of stone on the ground floor with big windows all around. And inside there's a swimming pool one of those heated ones. So you can swim even in winter and look out the window and see it raining and snowing. Beautiful things. Just beautiful. There's this other building as tall as a castle and it has glass all around too. That's where we have our parties. The floor is all parquet and I've put a table in there that goes all the way from one side to the other and seats thirty or forty people easy. There's a fireplace and a dance floor. And the best stereo system but of course we don't even need it since we'll have live music from Thomai. And then there's a special computer that splits the ceiling in two when I touch it and all the glass on the sides comes down. That's a trick for summer so we don't get too hot even though I've also put in the best air conditioner there is. On summer nights we gather up there and eat and drink as much as we want and dance until the sun comes up. And I'm sitting there in a corner watching you all having a great time and I'm so happy even though there's something burning me up inside. Because you guys don't know. You think I won millions in the lottery or something. That's what I told you. You don't know that I've found this magic potion that makes me invisible and I've been robbing banks without ever getting caught. And you also don't know that every time I drink that potion I lose a year off my life. That's the deal. Every time I drink the potion my life gets another year shorter. But you don't know anything about that. I don't ever let you find out. And we clink glasses and you make toasts to me, may the admiral live a thousand years. And I watch you from my corner and I'm so happy. I look at the kids having fun and I'm happy. I look around at all the things I built and I say, things are just fine. And when the party ends and you all go to sleep I get up and go down to the beach and sit all by myself and stare at the sea for hours. And I feel a sadness like you wouldn't believe because I've drunk a lot of that potion and I don't have much time left. And I think how in the end what I did is pretty cowardly. But I don't regret it. No. Because I've seen your faces and I know. I know that sometimes good doesn't walk the same road as truth. And I know that good is sometimes more important than true. I know.

He stopped talking but didn't open his eyes. His cheeks were yellow. Vayios looked at us and pursed his lips and shook his head. He pushed the admiral's glass to the far edge of the table and gestured to Satanas, who came out from behind the bar and picked up the chair Iraklis had knocked over and then came over to us. He tore at a rib with his teeth.

What's going to happen with you assholes here every night, he said. Don't you guys have homes?

The admiral raised his head and looked at him. He blinked his eyes like a frightened animal.

Bring us another half kilo. And whatever the guys are drinking. And something else to snack on.

Satanas tossed the bone on the table and sniffed and leaned heavily on the admiral's chair.

What sort of snack would the gentlemen care for? He asked. We've got shrimp testicles stuffed with wild rice and crocodile saganaki with four kinds of cheese. Or perhaps you'd prefer something sweet? I prepared a special ice cream today with kangaroo milk and syrup from wild berries.

He looked at us and then at the admiral who had bowed his head again. He grabbed the admiral under the armpits and abruptly lifted him out of the chair.

Take him home, he said to Vayios. Get going. Get lost. Beat it already.

At the door he called to us and we turned around.

And listen. You'll have to invite me sometime to that estate for one of those parties, okay? I want to swim in that pool, too. Here's to you, Pavlakos, invisible bank robber. I'm expecting an invitation, you hear? Look at these guys. Just look at these guys, wanting villas and pools. He's a real number, that one. You all are.

. . .

Yesterday morning we found Mao's cat hanging from the mulberry tree in front of his house. They'd tied her up by her hind legs and thrown salt in her eyes. She was covered in blood. She'd clawed out her own eyes. By the time we found her the blood had dried on the sidewalk and flies had eaten half her head. The place stank.

We all stood around in a circle and looked without speaking. Only the deafmute tried to say something with his hands but no one was paying attention so he left.

Michalis untied the cat from the branch and wrapped her in newspaper and went to throw her in the field behind the church of Osia Xeni.

When the crowd dispersed Michalis's mother brought a bucket and mop and started scrubbing the blood off the sidewalk. She kept murmuring to herself and wiping her eyes with the sleeve of her jacket.

Poor Mao, she said. What did those awful people do to you. My strong young man. Poor Mao.

And a Kinder Egg For the Kid

HUNGER WOKE HIM. He'd had a pain in his belly all night. He had his son with him, too. His son was sleeping beside him in the bed with his mouth open and his fingers gripping the edge of the blanket as if he had fallen asleep afraid that someone might try to take the blanket away. He turned over slowly and propped himself on his elbow and looked down at his son. The kid looked nothing like him. Nothing at all. For starters, the boy was blond. Not blond blond but still blond. And he was very beautiful, with a narrow face and eyes the color of the sky when a north wind is blowing. He had a little mole under his right eye. In the dark the blond fuzz by his ear shone as if all night someone had been stroking him right there with fingers covered in gold dust. The kid was so beautiful that it hurt his heart to look at him. And yet he couldn't get his fill of looking, he looked and forgot his hunger. When he grows up. When he grows up he'll look at me and ask why I had to be his father why he had to grow up in a place like this and sleep in a bed like this. Why. Why.

He closed his eyes. That pain again. He felt a movement in his belly as if there were something alive in there.

Dad?

The kid was awake and looking at him with blurry eyes.

Dad we have to eat something. Our stomachs are growling.

The kid lifted his head off the pillow and something white glistened at the corner of his mouth. Milk. Only it wasn't milk. It was dried spit.

Go back to sleep. It's still early. He stroked the kid's hair, forced a smile. I'm going out now. Are you listening? I don't want you to be scared. I'm going out now for a little while. And when you wake up the table will be set and we'll eat and eat until Easter Monday. Okay? High five.

The kid closed his eyes and licked his lips and said I'm hungry and squeezed his eyes tightly shut and didn't say anything else.

. . .

Sir, the girl said. Would you put the crown on our Jesus's head?

. . .

He'd been walking since noon and now it was evening and he was still walking. Nikaia Neapoli Korydallos Nikaia Neapoli Korydallos – tracing circles like a caged animal like that wolf he'd seen once when he was a kid running around and around in its cage at the zoo and that night he'd stayed up crying thinking of that wolf that was just skin and bones with its dirty matted fur running around in its cage with a crazed look in its eyes. And he'd asked his father who said the wolf was running because wolves are born to run and if you shut a wolf up in a cage it's as bad as killing it. And he'd asked his father if he could do something, if he could unlock the cage and let the wolf out and his father looked him in the eye for a long time – it was the only time he remembered his father giving him that kind of look – and then started to say something but in the end he didn't.

He'd cried for many nights over that wolf. Many nights and plenty of afternoons too.

Thursday before Easter and a poisoned wind was blowing, the trees thrashed in the wind as if some huge invisible hand were shaking them. He walked and his mind was on the kid who must have woken up hours ago and would be sitting at the kitchen table with his hands folded together dreaming with open eyes of a table spread with food. He was walking to kill time, until ten when he was going to meet his daughter at the port. She was headed down from Thessaloniki to take the boat to Rhodes to spend Easter with her mother. He hadn't seen his daughter in two years and tonight he would be seeing her and was planning on asking her for money. Fifty euros. Fifty euros would be plenty. Pasta a little cheese bread milk. Beer. A bottle of ketchup which the kid liked. And a chocolate egg, one of those Kinder ones – a treat for Easter. Fifty euros would be plenty. He thought about how his daughter would look at him when he asked her for money and what she would say to him and what she would say to her mother when she got to Rhodes. I can't believe it, mom. He asked me for fifty euros he said he doesn't have any money at all says they don't have money for food.

He walked and felt his face reddening with shame and felt the hunger and the shame gnawing at his guts like starving rats.

Fifty euros, he said – and a woman passing beside him looked at him in fear.

Fifty euros would be plenty.

With fifty euros we'll have a fine Easter.

. . .

Sir, the girl said. Would you put the crown on our Jesus's head?

. . .

Eighty-five people lost their jobs when the Roter factory in Renti closed. Women and men. Young people and old people and contract laborers from the Greek Manpower Employment Organization. At first he ran around like everyone else – to government ministries, political parties, protests, demonstrations. Slogans, banners, raised fists, voices hoarse from shouting. Rage, fear, anxiety. The worst were the words, the rumors, the lies. First they raised your hopes and then they cut the legs out from under you, beat you, destroyed you. That was the worst. The words, the lies. At some point he got tired and lost hope and started to look for other work. Then people heard they were going to be transferred to the surrounding municipalities for part-time employment. And he was happy and hopeful again and told the kid not to worry, everything was going to be fine, have faith in your father. Weeks passed. And then he found out that the positions had already been assigned.

The positions have been assigned, they told him. The municipalities had been parceled out by party. The communists got Kokkinia, New Democracy got Korydallos and Keratsini, the right-wingers went all over. Everyone landed somewhere. Except for him and five or six others who hadn't known. Who didn't get there in time. Who weren't red or green or blue. It all happened quietly, simply, beautifully. And he never heard a thing.

He and five or six others.

They sold us down the river, the others said. Don't you get it, you fool? Our co-workers. Our comrades-in-arms. They sold us out.

That all happened in February. On the last Sunday of Carnival there was a big party in the federation offices. Everyone brought food from home and sweets and wine and beer. Three or four brought bouzoukia and guitars so there would be singing and dancing. They hung banners on the walls. *Our struggle*

is bearing fruit. Never swerve from the road of class struggle.
Strength in unity, victory in struggle, solidarity as our shield.
Those were the kinds of banners they'd hung on the walls. He
went right when it started and sat at a distance from the others
and drank. He watched them eating pickles and hard-boiled
eggs, cheese pies and spinach pies. They ate off of aluminum
foil, drank wine out of Coke and Sprite bottles. They clinked
plastic cups and laughed and clapped and danced the zeibekiko.
He watched them with hatred and jealousy. He watched them
without wanting to. As if he were a dead man who had been
allowed to return for a brief while to the land of the living, to
walk invisible among the living until he was pulled back again
into death – a terrible punishment.

Later on, when he'd drunk a lot and his fear had faded, he got
to his feet and started speaking loudly. He said things he'd been
wanting to say for a while – for months, even years. He said
things he'd thought about many times and other things he'd
never thought until that instant. There were moments when he
felt as if the voice that was speaking weren't his, as if the person
speaking weren't him. At first they watched him with curiosity.
Then they looked at him with pity. Some laughed. Others kept
eating. Some pushed back their chairs and walked out. There
were moments when his voice faded and his eyes burned and a
knot rose in his throat. There were moments when he imagined
himself sitting on the other side of the room and listening and

78

shaking his head with pity. In the end someone shouted at him to shut up and get lost – throw out the apolitical bullies, the guy shouted, throw out the provocateurs. Someone grabbed him by the arm and told him to sit down. Get a hold of yourself and sit down. Now. He sat. And then he jumped back up to his feet and rushed forward and took tables chairs cups people with him as he fell and as he fell time stopped inside him and he seemed to be falling very slowly from the sky and could see the pattern on the floor as if it were the whole earth which from that height was so beautiful – mountains, fields, streams – that his heart swelled from all that beauty and he laughed and shouted with joy.

And then someone hit him hard on the head and he tumbled once and for all to the floor.

· · ·

Sir, the girl said. Would you put the crown on our Jesus's head?

· · ·

At the corner of Kondyli and Ephesus he stopped in front of the Anemone sweet shop and looked in the window at the huge chocolate eggs and chocolate bunny rabbits and tsourekia covered in dark chocolate and slivered almonds. His heart was trembling even more than his legs. He stood in front of the window and looked at the tsourekia and his mouth filled with saliva. As soon as he got the fifty euros from his daughter he could take something else off of the list – the cheese, for instance – and get a chocolate-covered tsoureki instead. The kid would be so happy, he was crazy about chocolate. Though even he was shaking now as he gazed longingly at the sweets glistening in the light of the shop window and they looked so fresh so delicious so airy and wonderful. The things that make a person happy, he thought. A tsoureki covered in chocolate.

He started walking down Kondyli again toward the bridge. The wind had picked up. Women in black were walking on the sidewalk leaning into the wind and holding the edges of their coats to keep the wind from blowing them open. He heard church bells ringing in deep, heavy mourning and it struck him as strange because he knew there wasn't a church around there and for a moment, unconsciously, he stopped and looked up and started to cross himself – then immediately caught himself. He walked on with his head down staring at his boots which were covered with mud and dirt and looked like small black animals that had just emerged into the world from some burrow deep in the ground. He turned right on Antioch Street and then on Grevena and turned right again and looked at the building of the town hall which was tall and grey and he thought how small he would seem if someone looked at him from up there. He stopped in front of the Bank of Greece and took his ATM card out of his wallet and put it in the machine and pressed the buttons and closed his eyes for a few seconds and said something on the inside as if he were a man of faith who prayed every Good Thursday in front of an icon of the crucified Christ and then he opened his eyes and saw on the screen a tiny little person looking at him with hands raised – *we're sorry we can't complete that transaction* – and pulled his card from the machine and put it back in his wallet which was black and empty and then he turned and left.

He crossed the street and turned onto Tsaldari and held his breath as he walked in front of the kebab stand and turned left and stopped in front of the Galaxy Supermarket and looked at the people shopping or waiting in line to pay and he was suddenly gripped by dizziness and panic because it occurred to him that at ten when he met his daughter the supermarkets would already be closed so where would he buy the pasta and cheese and milk and the Kinder egg for the kid and he looked at the business hours posted in the supermarket window and saw that tonight it was closing at nine and his panic grew and he leaned against a parked car and told himself to calm down, said it three times like a prayer – calm down calm down calm down – then went and stood on the corner of the street where there was a bitter orange tree with no bitter oranges on it and he pulled off a dusty leaf and crushed it between his fingers and smelled his fingers to try and pull himself together but all they smelled like was dust and sweat and fear.

Then a sudden gust of wind blew and a black garbage bag leapt up from the sidewalk and wrapped itself around his legs and for a moment he froze as if there were a black snake on his legs and then he shook his legs and started to kick at the air to get the bag off and he kicked the air and shook his hands and legs and on the sidewalk across the street an old woman stopped and looked at him and shook her head sadly and crossed herself – Good Thursday evening and a north wind was blowing and the sky was the color of the kid's eyes who had been sitting for hours now at the kitchen table with his hands together dreaming with open eyes of a table covered with food. And it wasn't winter, it hadn't snowed, so he couldn't even go outside and break off an icicle hanging from the edge of the roof and lick it to trick his hunger into thinking it was being fed. It was spring, and it hadn't snowed around there in ten years.

· · ·

Sir, the girl said. Would you put the crown on our Jesus's head?

· · ·

When he got to the dock the digital clock on the stern of the ship said ten to nine and when he stubbed out his last cigarette the clock said ten past ten and his daughter was still nowhere to be seen. He stood up from the bench and circled the cars that were waiting in line to board the ship and then weaved between the cars looking at all the drivers and passengers. He scanned the people walking over the gangplank onto the ship and those few people leaning over the railing at the stern, to the right and left of the flagpole, looking down at the other people and at the cars and trucks.

At twenty-five past ten he asked someone wearing a white shirt with blue letters that read *BLUE STAR 2* if he could go up onto the ferry.

At twenty to eleven he bummed a cigarette off a truck driver and smoked it watching the stars flickering in the sky and said things about his daughter. Vulgar awful things. Things he had never said, things he didn't know a father could say about his own daughter.

At ten past eleven the ship loosed its moorings and pulled shuddering away from the dock with thick black smoke pouring out of its funnel. He stood there waiting until the lights on the ship were one tiny light way off in the sea. Then he turned to leave and saw something on a bench and went over to see what it was. A Coke with a straw in it and a half-eaten cheese pie. He glanced around and picked up the cheese pie. He smelled it.

Then he wrapped it in the paper and put it in his pocket.

He went out of gate E1 and headed back walking sometimes in the street and sometimes on the sidewalk and as he passed under the bridge he read something scrawled on the wall in black spray paint – *kick a nigger and ruin your boot* – and saw the lights of a truck coming slowly in his direction and thought about jumping into the middle of the street and standing there and letting the truck run him over so he could put an end to all this once and for all and then he stepped back and pressed his back against the wall of the tunnel and spoke to his body as if his body were a dog and he were its owner and he stayed like that with his back to the wall until the truck passed in front of him and drove off.

Then he thought about the kid. He imagined the kid being given his dead father's clothes and the kid taking them and stroking them with eyes full of tears and as he stroked them he would feel something hard in there and would stick his hand in the coat pocket and pull out a half-eaten cheese pie. How ridiculous that would be. How ridiculous.

. . .

After midnight he went up Cyprus Street walking on the left-hand sidewalk and when he got to the church of Osia Xeni he looked across and saw light and shadows behind the yellow pane in the door and crossed the street and went inside.

Six or seven women in black and a girl about eleven years old were decorating the bier with flowers. They were standing around the bier choosing flowers one by one from big bunches and cutting off the stems and sticking the flowers in the styrofoam. Daisies. Roses. And other flowers whose names he didn't know.

84

They turned and looked when he came in and kept looking as he sat down in a chair and crossed his arms over his chest and smelled the air which smelled like incense and human breath. He raised his eyes without lifting his head and looked at the enormous figure staring down at him from up in the dome and looked at the other figures painted on the walls and the purple ribbons and the icons and the candles burning and melting and bending over in the empty air like tired bodies looking for something to lean against.

Beside the bier was the cross. A big tall cross made of dark wood. Christ had his eyes closed and his head was lolling to the right. Arms bent at the elbows, legs bent at the knees. The nails in his hands dripped blood. A gash in his right side was bleeding, too. He turned his head away and closed his eyes then opened them again and looked back at the crucified figure. How peaceful he was. Peaceful. Calm. Resigned.

He looked once more at the women. He would ask them for money. Of course. He would ask them to give him some money. Five or ten euros each. Whatever you can. So I can feed my child. However much you like. Happy Easter to you all. They couldn't possibly refuse. Not for me. For my child.

Sir, said the girl. Would you put the crown on our Jesus's head?

She had come over to him and was standing there staring at him. Eleven or twelve years old. Big eyes, thick lips, blond fuzz on her cheeks. He reached out a hand to touch the fuzz on the girl's cheeks and the girl looked at his hand and grabbed his thumb and wrapped her hand around it.

It's too high we can't reach.

The crown was sitting on a table. He thought it was a crown of flowers but it wasn't. It was made out of some plant with thorns and in the shadowy light of the chandelier and the candles the crown looked like the skeleton of some strange soiled creature that had died on that table years ago.

He pulled a chair over in front of the cross and picked up the prickly crown as carefully as he could and climbed up on the chair and raised his hands to pass the crown over the top of the cross. The women and the girl were watching him. He turned around and looked at them and smiled.

What would you have done without me, he said. I hope you'll give me something for my trouble, he said and laughed.

The crown was small and he had to push to get it down over the cross and he could feel the thorns pressing into his palms but it didn't hurt. He looked into the face of Christ which was at the same height as his. Peaceful. Calm. Resigned.

Sure, he said. Since you know you'll be resurrected. Death isn't real, he said. Nothing is real. It's all just a show.

Evil's first victory is when it starts speaking your language, he said – and that scared him because he knew he wasn't capable of thinking or saying a thought like that. He looked at the crucified Christ, looked all around. Who had spoken. Who.

He stumbled on the chair and nearly fell. A woman screamed. He looked down at his hands. They were dotted with small perfectly round balls of blood. As if his hands were two shattered thermometers, thermometers that took the temperature not with mercury but with blood.

He turned and showed his hands to the women.

Look, he said. Look what happened. Now you definitely have to give me something for my trouble.

The women dropped their flowers and scissors and ran for the door. One grabbed her purse which was hanging on the back of a chair and hugged it to her chest as if it were an infant. Another grabbed the girl by the arm and ushered her out the door. They all left without looking back.

Don't go, he shouted. Wait. Don't.

He stepped forward into the air and fell to the floor and heard something snap and lay there motionless.

Wait.

Outside the wind was dying down and the clouds were motionless in the sky.

It was early on Good Friday morning.

The kid must have fallen asleep still hungry at the kitchen table.

A lump had caught in the throat of the day.

Any moment now it would start to rain.

Placard and Broomstick

At dawn the sky was full of tiny scattered clouds as if there had been some awful explosion up there. Yiannis Englezos looked at himself in the mirror splashed cold water on his face combed his fingers through his hair looked in the mirror again and pinched his cheeks to give them some color. He hadn't slept in four days for four whole days he hadn't closed an eye, and now in the darkness of the day and the frigid air of his apartment he felt something inside him getting very small, shrinking and drying up and turning black like a peppercorn.

He was a grocery stocker at the Galaxy Supermarket on Kaisareia Street, the first to open in Nikaia.

Liar, he told the mirror. Cowardly liar.

It was the second-to-last thing he would say that day.

· · ·

In the kitchen he put on some coffee and looked out the window. It was the Monday after Easter. Christ had risen twice but outside nothing had changed. Darkness and cold, it looked like it might rain, more like Good Friday than Easter Monday.

He went back into the living room and took up the task he'd left half finished. He pulled sixteen A4-sized cardboard dividers out of some folders and glued them together into pairs, which he spread out on the threadbare carpet to form a rectangle that measured 84 by 59.4 centimeters. He taped the eight double pieces together, turned the whole thing over and taped them again, then grabbed the red broomstick and wiped it down with a cloth, slowly and carefully, like a veteran hunter sitting beside the fireplace late one winter night, cleaning his gun and gazing into the flickering flames and wondering how so many years had passed without him noticing and how he himself had become not hunter but prey.

When he finished with that, he squeezed a long line of glue onto the cardboard then pressed the broomstick into the glue and counted to seventy. He cut four lengths of red string, twenty centimeters each, made eight holes in the cardboard, to the left and right of the broomstick, passed the string through the holes and tied it around the broomstick to strengthen the whole contraption. He looked at his makeshift placard and lit a cigarette. He smoked it down to the filter and each time he inhaled he could feel the smoke chafing his throat – he must have smoked an entire carton over the past four days. He waited a little while then held the stick up high and waved it around to see if the cardboard would hold. It was shoddy work. But with things as they were it was the best he could do. With things as they were he couldn't wait.

He lit another cigarette and lay down on the carpet with his knees bent in the air. He heard the churchbells start to ring and thought how crazy it was to eat the body of Christ and drink the blood of Christ and as he smoked he looked out at the day that refused to be anything but black that refused to sweeten even a drop.

. . .

On the Thursday before Easter Petros Frangos, his best and only friend, had been killed at a building site on Papadiamantis Street, a stone's throw from the old cemetery in Nikaia. He was electrocuted. He wasn't actually killed there because he didn't die right away. He died two days later, on Good Saturday, in the intensive care unit of a state-run hospital. He was an experienced steelworker, knew his trade, one of the last Greeks in that line of work. And on that day, Good Thursday, the contractor had pressured Petros to stay late and work into the evening – what with Easter and all the state holidays they were falling behind on the job. Petros said fine but it wasn't fine. He was in a hurry to finish up because that evening they were supposed to leave for Yiannis's village. They were going to spend Easter together up in the mountains of Epirus. You're going to take me with you this time, he'd told Yiannis. There's no way I'm staying down here for another Easter. I want to try it out, he'd said, to see what it's like because I can't stay here much longer, man. Things here are getting rough, everyone's losing it, these days people scare me. You tell me the only thing that makes life worth living is giving yourself to others. But what happens if no one wants to take? What if you don't find anyone to give yourself to? I'm telling you, the future is in the mountains – that's the kind of crazy stuff he'd been saying to Yiannis.

Give us the mountains, he said, even if we have to eat stones.

Like what Kolokotronis said during the revolution. Give us Greece even if we have to eat stones.

And then as he was carrying steel reinforcing bars that night one of them brushed up against a high-voltage wire and twenty-four thousand volts shot through Petros and shook his body and tossed him down on the dusty cement as if he were already dead or something that was never alive to begin with.

Not even water, he'd told Yiannis. In two years we won't even have water to drink. They said it on the news. That's why I keep telling you, we have to head for the mountains. I can't stand it here any longer. I'm sick of always being caught unawares. In this city every new day and every new person is another kick in the teeth.

Or a cracked reinforcing bar, to say it in my language.

. . .

He didn't die right away. He died on Good Saturday in the intensive care unit of a state-run hospital in Nikaia. Everything inside of him was burnt, the doctors said. The skin had come loose from the bottom of his feet and they looked like shoes with no soles. During those two days they let Yiannis in to see him three or four times and each time he had to put on a mask and gloves and plastic booties over his shoes – a new, warm pair of boots, with solid soles that hadn't yet been worn down – and each time he stood by the side of the bed he saw Petros's arm or foot suddenly flail, two or three or four times in a row, and Yiannis's eyes would fill with tears and to steel his nerves he would repeat words to himself from some old prayers that he had mostly forgotten. But that flailing wasn't the work of god. It was just the current shaking Petros's body – that's how much current was still in his body.

At night to keep himself from falling asleep he did arithmetic on cigarette packs. He divided 24,000 by Petros's age to see how many volts there had been for each year of his friend's life. He multiplied Petros's age by 365 and divided that into 24,000 to figure out the volts per day. Then he calculated the hours and the minutes and the seconds. That's how he spent his nights.

And when he got tired of numbers he wrote other things.

Caution! Keep away from the patient! He's a shocker!

What's black and red and jumps in bed? Petros!

You have a body like an electric eel vai vai vai vai vai dance the tsifteteli.

Hahahahaha, Yiannis wrote on his cigarette packs.

Hahahahaha.

. . .

Do something, he told the doctors. I don't have money now but I'll get some. I swear to you, I'll get some. If you could just save him. We've been together since we were kids. You know how it is. You've got friends you've known since you were kids, don't you? Please, I'm begging you. Do something.

. . .

He found a thick black marker and kneeled on the rug and wondered what he should write on the cardboard. He wanted to write something that would express unspeakable rage and hatred and love and despair all at once. Or maybe it should be some plain, dry slogan, the kind of thing a political party might say about workplace fatalities, about people who die on the job. Or maybe something like the things they write on the gravestones of people who die in vain, or too young. Something about god and the soul and angels and the afterlife.

He wondered if he should write something not about Petros but about Yiannis.

I'm filled with an incredible emptiness.

The other day on TV they were talking about some guy in America or Canada who got fired and two days later went back to the factory with a load of rifles and pistols and mowed down anyone who got in his way then blew his own brains out and on the t-shirt he was wearing those words were written in big black letters, that exact phrase.

I'm filled with an incredible emptiness.

What an insane thing to say.

. . .

In the bathroom he got his hair wet and slicked it back and carefully covered the shiny spot on the top of his head and put on his hat. It was a light hat of soft black leather but when he put it on and looked in the mirror he felt as if he were wearing a helmet.

He went back into the living room and picked the placard up off the rug and looked at the cardboard which still had nothing written on it and twirled the broomstick in his hand and then put the cap back on the marker and set it down on the coffee table and looked at the walls around him and with his free hand grabbed his hat and pulled it down low over his forehead like a man leaving a place forever, never to return, and –

Enough, he said and went out into the street.

. . .

The clouds had grown bigger and were casting long shadows over the city and from up there on the hill the city lay spread before Yiannis's eyes like a dirty wrinkled blanket. He headed towards Neapoli walking in the street next to the sidewalk with the placard on his shoulder and as he walked he looked at the ashen sky and remembered a documentary he'd seen a while back on TV about some rich English or Irish guy – he never really figured out where the guy was from, it was late and he was dozing on the sofa – who'd had an asteroid or something named after him. They showed the guy saying how proud and happy he was about that, about them giving his name to an asteroid – I like thinking that even when I die, he said, my name will keep orbiting the universe for years, even centuries. And Yiannis walked with the placard on his shoulder looking at the sky and thinking how strange it would be for them to name an asteroid Petros, if instead of that foreign guy it had been Petros, if it were the name Petros that would orbit for whole centuries through the universe, an asteroid, a small lonesome planet.

What's wrong with you, he said to himself. You know that could never happen.

Who would give a steelworker's name to a planet or an asteroid or even a meteorite.

Then he remembered what he'd said to the doctors. Please,

do something, save him, please. Do something. What a fool he'd made of himself. Instead of grabbing those assholes by the scruffs of their necks and pummeling them, instead of turning the whole place upside down, he'd sat there and cried and pleaded and scribbled on packs of cigarettes. And the jerks had made a fool of him, too. We're doing everything we can. It's a challenge for us just to keep your friend alive, they told him. Sure. A real challenge. Then again why would they show you any respect. Money. That was the real issue. Money. They didn't think you could come up with the cash. If you'd waved it in their faces they would have done something. They would have found some way to save him. You should have given them twenty-four thousand euros. One for each volt. Twenty-four thousand, sure, you don't even have twenty-four in your pocket. Worthless fool. Lying coward.

It was unfair, though.

He thought how unfair it was that the only words he had found to say to the doctors seemed to have come straight out of some series on TV. Then it occurred to him that now that he'd started to talk the way people talk on TV he might start to think like them too and that thought terrified him, it froze his heart – and then he stood up tall and gripped the broomstick in his hand and walked faster and consoled himself with the thought that no one on any TV series would ever do what he was doing today.

Then again he couldn't be sure. Because it's a proven fact that people on TV have great imaginations.

. . .

He walked down Attaleia to Papadiamantis turned right walked past Philippou and when he got to the corner of Papadiamantis and Palamas he stopped. The entrance to the building site was blocked by a chain-link fence. He looked at the wires hanging overhead and wondered which one had killed Petros, which was the wire with the twenty-four thousand volts. Then he stood with his back to the entrance and held the placard in the air with both arms. He stood between sacks of cement and barrels of lime between stacked crates and steel and piles of bricks. Across from him was a row of apartment buildings that stretched from one corner of the street to the other, an unbreachable rampart. He knew that the contractor, Petros's boss, lived in one of those buildings, and he held his placard up high so it would show. The street was deserted, there wasn't a soul on any of the balconies. He held the placard high and waited. Someone would come for sure. Someone would notice him, someone from the neighborhood would come down the street and stop and ask him what was going on why he was standing there holding a broomstick with that piece of cardboard on it and Yiannis would explain to him and the other guy would say yes, he'd heard about the man who'd been electrocuted the other day but he didn't know he had died and he would shake his head and tell Yiannis to take courage what can you do in this life what can you say that's how life is and the hardest part is for those who are left behind and he would ask how old Yiannis's friend had been and if he'd had a wife and kids and siblings and if his mother and father were still alive – and in a half-hour at most the whole neighborhood would have heard that a guy with a hat and a sign was standing in front of the building site and people would come out onto their balconies to see and would speculate and gossip, what kind of weirdo is he maybe a thief or a pederast waiting to swipe some kid? Go inside and call the police.

. . .

He wouldn't tell them his real name. He would make up some other name, more suited to the circumstance, a nice heroic name.

My name is Achilles. Achilles Palaiologos.

Or Alexander. Or Thrasyvoulos. Alexander the Great Thrasyvoulos Nikiforidis.

. . .

Someone would come and ask him about the placard and all the rest. For sure. Maybe some kid or old woman in black who knew a thing or two about death. Or maybe some drunk. Easter

Monday was a holiday and on holidays people are different, they soften and open up and care about others about their fellow man.

Someone would come for sure.

Even if only out of pity.

It was Easter Monday, Christ had risen twice.

Someone would come.

And that someone might even bring him a piece of cold lamb to eat, a little wine or a red egg.

. . .

At three a car turned the corner. The man at the wheel slowed down and looked at Yiannis with his mouth hanging open, the way drivers on the highway stare at traffic accidents.

Then he stepped on the gas and left.

. . .

A piece of tape came loose from the cardboard and dangled in the air like a yellow tongue. He turned the placard on its side and stuck the tape back on, pressing it firmly with his thumb. It was shoddy work. If only he'd written something surely someone would have paid attention someone would have stopped out of curiosity to ask him what it was all about. It would have been better than nothing. But he couldn't write anything. All the things he had inside, everything he was feeling, were like these fish he'd seen once on TV, strange fish that live deep down in a lake in Asia somewhere and when you take them out of the water and the sun hits them they rot right away and dissolve and disappear.

He couldn't write anything on the cardboard.

There are certain things it's hard to pull out from inside. Very hard. Impossible.

It's like asking someone to cry from only one eye.

. . .

At four he saw a woman in the building across the street sneaking peeks at him from behind a curtain. When she saw him looking back at her the woman made a face as if she'd just discovered a stain on the carpet and yanked the curtain closed.

At five he wondered if there's life after death and if Petros might be watching him now from somewhere, if he could see him standing there at the entrance to the building site with his hat on and the sign in his hands, and if with the wisdom of the dead Petros could possibly read all the things that Yiannis should have written on the cardboard.

Around five-thirty he thought: Petros died and nothing in the world can change that. Petros died and that won't change anything in the world. How does a person face that. How.

The most frightening thing isn't death but memories.

. . .

By evening it had started to rain.

One of the pieces of cardboard fell loose from the others and dropped to the ground and immediately shriveled up and turned black as if some kind of toxic fluid or poison had dripped on it.

He raised his collar and pulled his hat down low on his forehead and walked up and down for a little while to get warm looking at the deserted street, at the houses with lighted windows that seemed to be just as empty as the ones with no lights, looking at the black wires hanging overhead that emitted a constant hum as if they were relaying messages from a strange world to some other world. He circled the block then came back to his spot and stood there stiff as a rod holding the broomstick in both hands.

This, he thought, is the most pathetic, most ineffectual protest since the birth of the worker's movement. Since the birth of the world.

I'm filled with an incredible emptiness.

If only I had written something.

I'm filled with an incredible emptiness.

If I had written some heroic words of mourning someone would have paid attention.

For sure.

But now it's too late.

· · ·

Late at night he lit a cigarette without putting the placard down. Then he inhaled deeply and straightened his back and lifted the placard which was falling apart and held it high and kept on holding it high, with both hands, even as he exhaled and saw the smoke coming thick and yellow from inside his chest and watched it slowly rise under the yellow street light and then disperse in the darkness like the smoke from some pitiful ancient offering that no one even noticed, neither gods nor people who believed in gods.

The Blood of the Onion

I USED TO WORK IN KAMINIA at a factory that made ice. I checked the machines, tossed the ice into sacks, carried the sacks out to the truck. An easy job, ludicrous, a job to be ashamed of. But Michalis, the guy who did the deliveries, saw it differently. He said there were few jobs as difficult as this one. He would grab one of those ice cubes with a hole in the middle – for some reason we called them crooks – and close his palm around it. Within seconds it would begin to melt. In a minute or two it was water. In five it had disappeared.

Isn't that awful, he would say to me. To make something you know will be gone the very next moment. What an inhuman thing.

Shut up, Mike, I would say. Just stop thinking and work. Then I'd go to haul a few of those ten-kilo sacks we sent out to bars and restaurants. And he would trail after me somber and obedient as always looking at the palm of his hand which was bright red with cold.

Mi corathon, he would say. Mi corathon una naranha helada.

. . .

Ten months on the job and he still hasn't adjusted. He's a little off in other parts of his life, too. His folks died in a car accident when he was a kid. He'd been raised by some aunts out in the countryside. Later on he went to Romania to study medicine but came back after the first year—moneywise he couldn't make it work. He wanted to be a pediatrician and open his own practice. But his biggest dream was Spain. That was his goal, to go there one day and not come back. I'm not from here, he used to say, I'm from Spain. He'd taught himself Spanish from cassette tapes. He always said there was no other language like it. It's the happiest language in the world, he said, and when I finally get there I'll talk and laugh all day long. Even at the factory, all day he would toss out those mi corathons and naranha heladas. He didn't look anything like a Spaniard, though. You'd have thought he was from some northern country. Tall and blond, with green eyes and pale skin.

. . .

They'd hired him to be a driver but he did pretty much anything that came his way – electric stuff, plumbing, fixing the coolant. He learned fast, was quick on the uptake. He was a reader, too. He liked to read poems and used to carry a notebook around to scribble down all his strange thoughts. He saved and dreamed. He wanted to go back to Romania to finish his studies then head to Spain as soon as he was done. He said he'd find a Spanish woman with glossy hair and bright white teeth and they would travel the whole country together. They would go to where Don Quixote was from to see the windmills and the vineyards that stretched on as far as the eye could see. They would go down to the shores of the Guadalquivir and up to the Sierra Nevadas and to all those towns that Michalis had only seen on the map but whose names sounded so promising, Badajoz Almendralejo Villafranca de los Campaneros. Dreams. Dreams. For people like us dreams are like ice cubes – sooner or later they melt. But I never said anything.

Sometimes just to pass the time I'd ask him to tell me some poems. He knew lots of them, not just Greek but foreign ones, too. Of course he liked the Spanish ones best. There was one guy in particular, Miguel Hernández, whose name he said with a lisp, Hernándeth. He was crazy about that guy. He even had a photograph of him in his wallet, and knew his poems inside out, could say them by heart. Hernández had died young, when he was thirty or so. Most of his poems he'd written on toilet paper when he was in jail. He would tear the toilet paper into tiny pieces and write his poems on those little scraps. He was a communist and had fought in the civil war. After the war he was sentenced to death but he didn't live long enough to be executed, tuberculosis finished him off first. Michalis's favorite poem was Lullaby of the Onion. Apparently Hernández wrote it after he got a letter in prison from his wife where she wrote that she and their child – they had a baby boy eight months old – were living on nothing but onions and bread. They had nothing to eat except onions and bread. Onions and bread, that's how poor they were.

I don't know if all that was true or if Michalis just pulled it out of his head. But I can remember like it's happening now, him carrying sacks to the truck murmuring in his sad sing-song voice:

En la cuna del hambre
mi niño estaba.
Con sangre de cebolla
se amamantaba.

Mike, man, what's the guy trying to say, I asked the first time I heard it. What's all that cuna and staba about?

Michalis put the sack down and grabbed a piece of ice and held it in the palm of his hand and squeezed it tightly and as the ice melted, he told me that the poet was talking about his son – his niño – who was lying in the crib of hunger and nursing on the blood of the onion. Sangre de theboya means the blood of the onion, Michalis told me and as he said it his eyes were shining and you'd have thought he was on the verge of tears, as if it were his son lying in that crib, his son nursing on that strange blood.

Sangre de theboya. The blood of the onion.

Thpaniards, I told him. You're all crathy, every thingle one.

. . .

Lullaby of the Onion – that was Michalis's favorite poem. But I liked a different one, which Hernández wrote for his friend Ramon who died very young and very suddenly, so suddenly the poem said it was like a flash of lightning. I didn't know any Spanish or anything about poetry either. But I'd heard it so many times I'd learned a few lines by heart. I liked the part where Miguel said he wanted to dig up the earth with his teeth, to tear the whole earth apart so he could find his friend's bones and kiss them.

Quiero escarbar la tierra con los dientes
quiero apartar la tierra parte a parte

I liked the last lines, too. When Miguel tells the dead Ramon that one day they'll meet again and they'll have so much to say to one another.

Que tenemos que hablar de muchas cosas
compañero del alma, compañero

I liked that poem even though it was long and I couldn't remember most of the lines. I liked the sound of the words, their rhythm. I liked how Michalis said them. No pretense, just simply and sadly, the way you might read something you'd written a long time ago in some old notebook, a promise of undying love or friendship, some big statement you'd written about the future.

We have so many things to say
comrade of my soul comrade

. . .

It was January. Work was a bust. The boss had gone off again. He was a gambling addict like you've never seen, all the casinos from here to tomorrow knew his name. Parnitha Loutraki Thessaloniki you never knew where he'd be. He left a Palestinian in charge of the place while he was gone, Ziyad, who liked to play the tough guy. A shifty bastard who never smiled and had deep-sunk eyes and something threatening in the way he moved. He didn't have much give or take with anyone, kept us all at arm's length. Me in particular, there were plenty of times when I'd caught him looking at me like I was an Israeli soldier or something. Mark my words, I'd tell the others, things are going to get ugly with that guy. One day he's going to walk in here with dynamite strapped to his chest and blow us all sky high. Michalis saw things differently. He said that when he looked at Ziyad he saw the desert in his eyes. What desert, Mike? They have a desert over there? Of course they do – a huge one. He was sure that Ziyad had lived for years in the desert, and that's why he had that mysterious look in his eyes. Just look at him, he would say to me. Can't you see the guy isn't used to living among walls and machines? Don't you see how his eyes are searching for a little space to stretch out in? What could I say. I didn't see any desert in Ziyad's eyes, or any camels either. But there was one thing I saw: every time Michalis grabbed a piece of ice and let it melt in his palm Ziyad's eyes would flash with anger.

Michaliz! Don't mez the ize, man!

And Michalis would stop in his tracks and raise a fist in the air and intone the finest line of poetry he knew:

Ize cream youz cream we all zcream for ize cream.

We all laughed, but Ziyad didn't think it was funny. He would shake his finger and warn us.

If Kyrioz Giorgkoz come back you be the onez zcreaming.

And Michalis unfazed would answer again in poetry, lines by Michalis Ganas:

Poor Yiorgos
if only you could turn over
to see the other half of the world.

. . .

An unforgettable twentieth of January. We were loading up some orders for Piraeus. The day was so fine you could drink it from a glass. The Halcyon days. Of course now the whole year is one long Halcyon day, you can't even tell the difference. We were running behind because the Scot had gotten blocked up again. That's the name Michalis gave our biggest ice machine, not just because the brand was called Scotsman but also because when it got stuck it would only make half the ice it had been programmed to make. As stingy as a Scot, in other words.

I was struggling with the machine trying to get it going again. Ziyad had gone to put some money in the bank – he never trusted us with jobs like that. Michalis was stretched out in the shade reading a magazine he'd brought from home. He had a notebook open on his lap, too, and was scribbling something. I was about to start shouting when suddenly he let out a cry and leapt to his feet.

Come look at this.

I went over and he showed me the magazine. It was a special issue about the slogans written on walls from the time of the German occupation up to today. He pointed to a black and white photograph. On a wall was written: *Michael Ramos 19 years old address 11 Nemesis Street I will be executed 8-9-44.* And beneath, in capital letters: LONG LIVE THE FATHERLAND.

Michael, I said. Same name.

Look at the caption. Read the caption, man.

I read it.

Last words of a young man sentenced to death written on the walls of the Gestapo's basement cells on Merlin Street. A message with no recipient, written in the heat of the moment and therefore subjective, today it offers a cool, unprejudiced witness regarding the postmodern subjects of History.

Well, I said. Isn't that nice. Happy things. Now come and help with the Scot because al-Fatah will be back soon and we'll have him to deal with.

Michalis went over to the machine. I followed him. He bent down and took one of the few pieces of ice the Scot had spat out and held it in his hand. He squeezed it tightly until a trickle of water came out from between his fingers. Suddenly his face was bright red.

I don't understand, he said. What does it mean, a slogan written in the heat of the moment? He was nineteen years old. They were going to kill him at any minute. I mean, how was he supposed to be writing? Without a care in the world? Cool as a cucumber? And all that shit about unprejudiced witnesses and the postmodern subjects of history. What kind of person could write a thing like that? How can they be so. Just so. It's true, time is the worst healer. Time hardens people.

He hesitated for a minute and then said:

I want to swear. If you only knew how much I want to swear. But I can't. I can't even talk about it, you know? And since I can't say what I'm feeling I'm afraid I'll stop having those feelings. That they'll be lost. It's the silence that really scares me. It's inhuman. How much silence can a person carry inside?

He looked at me as if he were expecting an answer.

He opened his fist. The ice had melted.

It's your own heat of the moment now, I said. Come on, forget it. There's no making sense of things like that.

I felt his eyes burning my cheek. But he didn't say anything.

We stood with our arms crossed in front of the Scot. Now you could hear a strange, drawn-out hum like something in there was trying to get out.

I went inside and brought out a bottle of Johnny Walker from the holidays that I'd squirreled away. I filled two glasses. I scooped up a plastic cup of ice and every so often we'd toss another piece into our glass. We drank in silence, without clinking or saying cheers.

The sky was so blue it blinded you. The breeze smelled of the sea and french fries. What a beautiful day, I wanted to say. But I didn't. I thought about what Michalis had said. If you don't say what you're feeling at some point you stop feeling it. I thought about what it would be like to write *I will be executed* on a wall. What it's like to eat onions and bread day in and day out. To suckle on the juice of the onion and have the juice of the onion be blood. What it's like to work and save and dream and have those dreams melt like ice, as if there were special hands that existed in this world just for that – to hold the dreams of poor people and squeeze them until they melted like ice. But I didn't say anything.

Say something in Spanish, I told Michalis. I feel like laughing.

He took a piece of ice from his glass and held it in his palm and stretched out his arm.

With no recipient. No recipient back then and no recipient now.

That's not Spanish. I want to hear Spanish, man, get it? I want to hear corathon and theboya and muchas cosas. That's what I want to hear today.

The ice was melting in his palm. We watched the water seeping drip by drip between his fingers until it melted entirely, vanished. Michalis kept on holding his fist stretched out. His hair glinted gold in the sun. I saw him clenching his teeth. His jaw quaked.

Then there was a sound. The Scot suddenly came unblocked and the ice fell jangling into the bin like coins out of a slot machine.

The bin overflowed, the ice cubes started to drop onto the cement.

With no recipient, Michalis said.

The ice cubes kept falling.

We let them fall – we didn't even care.

Mi corathon. Mi corathon una naranha helada.

We drank and watched the ice fall onto the cement.

My heart. My heart a frozen orange.

Heaped on the cement, the ice cubes had already started to melt.

Something Will Happen, You'll See

ANOTHER NOTIFICATION came today from the bank. It says it's a final notification and that next week they'll take "actions permitted by law." They've called several times too but Niki never picks up. She set the letter on the coffee table in the living room. When Aris came home from work he saw it but didn't say anything. He didn't even touch it. He just stood and looked at it with eyes glazed from lack of sleep. Unshaven, in need of a haircut, his sideburns as long as a werewolf's. Then he took off his shoes and went into the bedroom and collapsed fully dressed onto the bed and pulled the sheet up over his head.

He's been lying there for three hours. Not speaking. Not moving. You'd think he even stopped breathing.

Niki loads the washing machine, then vacuums and mops. She gets down on all fours to pick up the broken glass from under the kitchen table. The floor smells of tsipouro. She douses it with disinfectant and scrubs until her fingers turn white and start to ache. Every so often she goes over to the bedroom door and looks at him, wondering how long he'll last.

You'll suffocate in there, she finally says. Come on out. You're not going to achieve anything that way.

No response. But Niki knows he's listening. His left leg is quaking under the sheet. As if he had no control over it – as if it were someone else's leg, not his.

You have to stay strong, she says. Something will happen, you'll see. Banks don't just take people's homes away. This isn't America. We'll manage somehow. You'll see.

Outside the sun is starting to set. The sunlight has cast an orange patch on the wall over the bed. Niki stares at it, wondering how she never noticed that orange patch on the wall before. She thinks how unfair it is that she doesn't know what to say to Aris, to make him understand how it feels to be seeing that patch on the wall for the very first time. Last night after helping him to bed she made herself some coffee and turned on the television. Recently she'd been having trouble sleeping and Aris was snoring so loudly that she knew even if she lay down she wouldn't be able to sleep. There was a documentary on about American Indians but Niki just stared out through the balcony door at the glow from the floodlights over at the electric plant. That afternoon a bunch of workers had climbed up on the chimney and hung a banner and shouted slogans. She watched the beams from the floodlights slicing the darkness like enormous swords and wondered how an artist would paint this scene – if there were still artists left in the world who

118

painted scenes like that: a woman sitting in the dark with a cup of coffee and a cigarette, her face lit by the dim blue light of the television. Wouldn't be much of a painting. Maybe if she had a gun in her hand, or a vibrator. Coffee and cigarettes wouldn't cut it. People don't get excited anymore about old-fashioned things. Who cares about the finances and family problems of the petit bourgeoisie? Très banal. She leaned over to stub out her cigarette and saw a girl on TV who looked like an Indian only she was wearing glasses and modern clothes and talking about the history of her tribe and saying that many many years ago the people of her tribe had been forced to leave their land and as they left some touched the leaves and branches as a way of saying goodbye and others touched the grass and the flowers and the water that bubbled from the springs and the pebbles on the riverbanks, and the soldiers who had come to force them out had watched this peculiar sight and laughed – they didn't know what it's like to have to leave a place you love, the girl said. The interviewer asked how she knew about all those things if they'd happened so long ago and the girl said that the truth of a story lies not in its adherence to the facts but in its moral character. When the documentary was over Niki turned off the television opened the balcony door and looked at the beams from the flashlights of the striking workers at the electric plant who seemed prepared to spend all night perched up there on the chimney and as she looked at the dark shapes of the brick buildings and the exhaust towers she remembered her mother saying that in her day all the doctors in that area used to tell new mothers not to breastfeed their babies because the air in those neighborhoods – Haravgi Drapetsona Keratsini – was full of fluorine from the fertilizer plant in Drapetsona and the fluorine got into their milk. Then she went into the bedroom and looked at her husband who was sleeping wrapped up in the sheet with his socks still on and she pulled a jacket over her shoulders and took her coffee and cigarettes and keys and went upstairs onto the roof of the building and looked down at the world spread out all around her. The port the ships the housing projects. The abandoned fertilizer plant the chimneys the water towers. The sky was full of stars and the moon was out but Niki didn't need any light to see – even with her eyes closed she knew where everything was. The cement factory the slaughterhouses the British Petroleum plant the church of Agios Nikolas. The fishing docks and the boatyards in Perama. In the distance was the industrial island of Psittaleia and then Salamina with its densely clustered neighborhoods: Paloukia Ambelakia Selinia. She grabbed hold of the railing and felt its rough metal scratch her palms. From where she stood she could see the memorial to the battle against the Germans at the electric plant in 1944 which was now surrounded by palm trees and she could see countless unnamed alleys and streets lined with bitter orange trees and mulberry trees and apartment buildings built side by side whose balcony awnings were torn by wind and blackened with age. Her gaze wandered back down to the cars and motorbikes and motorized tricycles and the yards in front of the refugee houses, yards with flowerpots and clothes strung up on lines and old useless things – a broken refrigerator, a bicycle missing its wheels, a three-legged chair, a crib with no slats. Then she looked back at the apartment buildings and at the lighted windows here and there and wondered if other people were up as late as she was tonight or if they'd left those lights on out of fear. And if they were still awake was it because of something good or something bad? And if they'd left the lights on out of fear what were they afraid of? Burglars, or something else? She lit a cigarette and drank her coffee which had grown cold and looked around again and wondered what she would do if one day she was forced to leave this place, the place where she was born and raised and became a woman. If she would go out into the street and say goodbye to the bitter orange trees and mulberry trees by touching their leaves and their branches. If she would touch all the park benches in all the squares and all the utility poles, plastered with posters and funeral announcements and *FOR RENT* signs. And the red Vespa still chained to the front gate of Thodoris Skoupas's yard, which he washed every Sunday morning while he was alive and then doused with cologne to make it smell nice. You'd think she was an Indian the way she would run her hands over the metal grate on Asterias's newspaper stand, which had been closed for years now – run and hide Asterias the anarchists are coming, the kids used to yell who hated him because of the big AEK team poster he'd hung behind the counter. She would touch the wall at the corner of Bosphorus and Mycenae Streets across from the school where a line of faded spray paint read *Vacation is the alibi for an eleven-month rape*. And the front gate of Voula's house that's been crooked since the night last year when her husband came home drunk and drove right into it. She would touch the window of Kosmas's barber shop where one afternoon twenty years ago she had seen a fifteen-year-old Aris sitting in the chair with his head bowed and his hair in tufts on the floor around him – and how dearly she wishes she could turn back time and sweep all that hair off the floor into her hands and smooth it back onto Aris's head.

There were so many things she would have to touch in farewell if one day she were forced to leave this place. Even if she isn't an Indian and there aren't soldiers to watch her and laugh even if there isn't anyone to tell her story on television.

And now she's standing at the bedroom door looking at Aris and that orange patch on the wall and remembering all the things she heard last night on TV. The truth of a story lies not in its adherence to the facts but in its moral character. She's not sure exactly what that means but she likes the idea that there might be true things that have never happened. She likes the

122

idea that there are things that are both true and not true. Things that may never have happened but are still truer than the truth. Then again she isn't sure. If only she could understand better. If only they had money and she didn't have to work. If only she could read more and travel and go to the theater and concerts. If only she could sleep until eleven and not have to wait before dawn at the bus stop and be ashamed of her job. More than anything she would like not to feel a shock of fear every time the phone rings or she sees a plain white envelope in the mailbox.

She lies down beside Aris and the bed squeaks.

Come on out, she says to him. I want to tell you something. It happened at work yesterday. You've never heard anything like it.

No reaction. Niki turns onto her back and closes her eyes. She brings the images to mind, tries to put them in order and make the lump in her throat go away. She lets her heart grow cold. The story she wants to tell is a love story and she knows that kind of story can't be told with a warm heart.

· · ·

Around eleven I take a cigarette break and Rita comes whirling into the room and says listen to this you're not going to believe what happened you're going to flip. What happened, I say. Did one of the doctors ask you out? You know how Rita's been dying to hook a doctor or an army officer ever since she was a girl. Shut up and listen, she says, this is for real. Earlier this morning they brought in this couple from the Korydallos prison in an ambulance. The girl was one of ours and the guy was a foreigner. Bulgarian or Romanian I don't know. A young couple. He got locked up and she went to see him during visiting hours. In a few days they were going to send him back to his country, to deport him, you know. So during visiting hours this girl takes a tube of glue out from somewhere some kind of superglue and smears it all over her hand and they stick their hands together just like that. See? So they could be together forever and she could always stick by her man. Can you believe it? They stuck their hands together with superglue so that no one could tear them apart. Unbelievable. Just imagine, the things that happen in this world. Isn't it crazy? And now they brought them here for the doctors to get their hands apart. They took them up to the second floor. You know, to that room where they put prisoners. They've even got a guard up there keeping watch. It happened just now. Can you imagine, gluing their hands together. I'll bet they're some kind of addicts. Good riddance, I say, we don't need their kind around here.

That's what Rita says and then she takes a few drags of my cigarette and goes back to work all annoyed because a guy on her floor keeps throwing up – goddamned old man she says, he's been running me ragged since morning.

Niki rolls onto her side and looks at Aris. Wrapped in the sheet, arms at his sides, his breath barely audible, like a whisper.

Did you get what happened? she asks him. They stuck their hands together with glue so that no one could tear them apart. What do you think of that?

She looks at the sheet which has taken on the shape of his face. Then she lifts her head and looks at the orange spot on the wall which is shrinking smaller and smaller as the sunlight fades. She reaches out a hand and touches it before it vanishes altogether. She takes a breath and closes her eyes again.

. . .

I take my bucket and mop and go up to the second floor. I don't know what came over me. I wanted to see them. I wanted to see how it was, I wanted to see them. That room for the prisoners is at the very end of the hallway by the bathrooms. There's a young policeman sitting in front of the door smoking and playing with his cell phone. He sees me coming with my gear and I figure he won't let me in – he looks me over from head to toe. He makes me wait for a while then waves me in as if shooing a fly.

The room has an iron door with a padlock and a single bed and a window with bars and screens. Just like a cell. We don't clean it much. I've probably only been in there two or three times. The young man is lying on the bed. Naked from the waist up with his eyes closed and his right hand on his chest. His left hand is joined to the right hand of the girl who's sitting next to him on the edge of the bed and staring out the window. I can't

125

see their hands because they're wrapped in gauze. Rita was right they're just kids. Twenty, twenty-two at most. But they don't look like addicts – at least not the girl. When I go into the room the guy opens his eyes and looks at me vacantly then sighs and shuts his eyes again. But the girl smiles and stands up. Her skirt has crept up over her knees and she smooths it down with her free hand. Her cheeks are bright red.

Sorry to bother you, I say. I won't be long.

I start cleaning taking my time in no hurry at all. Of course what is there to clean in there really. I keep on glancing over to see what they're up to trying to think of something to say. I think about asking if she's okay what the doctors said how long they're going to keep them in the hospital if they're going to operate stuff like that. I want to ask if it was her idea for them to stick their hands together what kind of glue she used what the guards and prison officials did when they found out. Like if they hit her or yelled at her. There are so many things I want to ask. But I'm afraid the guard might hear us talking and kick me out. Besides I figure they might not be in the mood to talk. She's having a pretty rough time as it is the last thing she needs is some cleaning lady she doesn't even know peppering her with questions.

As I'm mopping I hear the young man murmur something. The girl bends down and strokes his forehead and hair. Then she turns and asks in a whisper if I have any cigarettes. Of course, I whisper back, and pull out my pack. She takes one and lights it and puts it in the kid's mouth. I gesture to her to keep the whole pack. Take it, I say, I've got another downstairs. I ask her if they need anything else. If she wants me to call a nurse or bring them some water or something from the canteen. I tell her I've brought stuffed tomatoes from home and feta and bread but I don't know if the guard will let me give it to them.

We're fine, she says with a smile and blushes even more. Thank you so much. We're fine. Thank you.

And then a strange thing happens. There we are talking in whispers and gestures and she suddenly holds out her hand to me. I don't know why I hesitate. I don't know why but I hesitate to take her hand. It's true. I stand there like an idiot holding my mop and staring at the hand she's stretched out in my direction. It's a tiny hand, like a drop of water. White and thin.

The girl smiles but in a kind of crooked way. Like when you get an injection at the dentist's office that makes your mouth all numb and swollen. Then she leans towards me and –

Don't worry, she whispers. There's no glue on this one.

· · ·

The sunlight has faded even more now. Through the balcony door Niki sees the streetlights coming on with a cautious flut-

127

ter. The cars passing by in the street have their lights on now. The room grows darker, filling with a strange darkness that seems almost alive.

That's all, Niki says. Then I went downstairs and worked until three and came home. I wanted to tell you about it last night but last night you weren't in such great shape, as I'm sure you remember. Do you? Do you remember anything about last night? Falling asleep at the kitchen table? With your cigarette still burning? You almost lit yourself on fire.

Aris says something but his voice is swallowed up by the sheet.

What did you say? I can't hear you. Come on out from under there already.

Her hands are sweaty. She wipes them on the sheet and looks at her palms. Then at her fingers. For the first time she notices how yellow they are. She's been smoking too much recently. Her fingers seem smaller, too. It must be her imagination but she's terrified by even the thought that her body has started to fall apart, to shrink. In the past she would have laughed at the idea. She would have told Aris: look at this, my fingers are shrinking. I've actually been working my fingers to the bone. And they would have laughed. They would have put their hands together to see how much bigger his fingers were than hers. Then Aris would grab them one by one and tugged on them to make them longer. They would laugh and laugh. But now Niki is afraid. There are so many small tiny things that frighten her. And then there's that pain in her chest. As if something in there is broken. As if something in there broke or got knocked out of place. She can feel some hard thing hanging in her chest like a broken spring. She observes the lines carved into her palms. Too many to count. Straight and crooked and curved. Some like barbed wire others like uprooted trees. Still others cross one another and fade away, or stop suddenly like a road that dead-ends into nothingness.

You should have called the stations.

Aris has pulled the sheet down from over his head and is looking at her. White as a ghost, lips dry, eyes bloodshot. His hair sticking up on one side like the plume on the helmet of an ancient warrior emerging from a bloody battle.

About what?

You should have called the stations, Aris says and turns his face away. They'd kill for that kind of news. You know, human interest stories. They would have gone nuts. You should have called and told them to come to the hospital and then asked to be paid for giving them the scoop. They would have given you something for sure. Even a little would have helped in our situation. Better than nothing.

He rubs his eyes then slips his hands under his head. He stares up at the darkening ceiling.

Niki can't see his hands.

She gets up out of the bed and goes over to the balcony door. Now the sky is a dark violet color. She sees a few stars flicker and the lights of an airplane slowly disappear. The banner is still hanging from the chimney of the electric plant but tonight there are no floodlights or striking workers. The strike was deemed illegal, they said on TV. Tonight things are calm again. All that's left is the banner hanging from the chimney, a long, narrow white banner with red letters which if you saw it from a distance, from the sea, would look like a huge gauze bandage spotted with blood.

You should have called the stations, Aris says. Now it's too late.

Niki looks at her palms and brings that image once more to mind. The girl in the hospital. How she leaned forward with one hand stuck to the young man's and the other extended toward Niki. The thin white hand Niki was afraid to touch. She wanted to do something for that girl. Something, anything. But now there was no point. She'll learn to live with that. Compromise. All of life is one big compromise. We're all born of compromise, Niki thinks, out of that great silent yes that our parents say when they choose to bring us into this world. Which means that we all carry a kind of compromise inside us, in our blood. That's why all revolutions are destined to fail. Then she thinks how she shouldn't waste time thinking about things like that. She should think instead about where she's going to find the money that they need and about the bank and the house and Aris who is still lying under the sheet – unspeaking unmoving defeated. She thinks that if things go wrong, if they don't find some way, she'll take some superglue and stick one of her hands to Aris's and the other to the wall. That's what she'll do. Then let them come and try to kick her and Aris out of the house. This isn't America. They can come if they want. She and Aris will be waiting.

She might even call the stations.

In the distance she sees a boat steaming off with all its lights on. A woman walks by in the street pushing a baby in a stroller. Two men stand talking on the sidewalk. One is smoking and the other is carrying a fishing pole and a blue plastic bag.

And then she doesn't want to see anything or think anything anymore. She closes her eyes and leans on the glass of the balcony door and with her eyes closed listens to the darkness of the house spreading itself around her and listens to the heartless hum of cars down below in the street.

The Things They Carried

F IVE MEN had lit a fire outside the Social Security offices in Nikaia in the middle of a January night. They were retirees, former office workers or manual laborers, unshaven and down at the heels. They'd started gathering there at three in the morning so they'd be the first to see the doctors before the crowds came and the line stretched all the way to the sidewalk. They didn't know one another and didn't bother to introduce themselves – they had other things on their minds. Besides, their names didn't matter. What mattered was the order, that the order of the line be strictly maintained. Which is why each man thought of himself and the others as numbers in a list that would keep growing as the night advanced.

They were five men but also five numbers.

That was one of the things they had on their minds.

. . .

They had lit a fire on the sidewalk in front of the steps.

Winter, bitter cold, a night that seemed to stretch on forever.

It had rained early that evening and now the damp had turned to frost that sparkled like silver dust on all the parked cars. At first they paced up and down on the sidewalk to get warm, watching silently, with a kind of awe, as their breath rose into the darkness like smoke signals. Then the first man to have arrived, number one, who had cataracts and was almost blind in his right eye, had an idea. They could light a fire with some wooden pallets and cardboard boxes that were piled next to a dumpster on the street. The others agreed right away because they were all very cold. One of them remembered that on his way there he'd seen a bunch of barrels outside of a building site on the next street over. He suggested they bring a barrel over and light the fire in it. They agreed to that, too, because they needed some way to keep the fire going until morning – that was another thing they had on their minds.

Two of the men went to get the barrel, revolving it heavily over the sidewalk, and set it in front of the steps of the Social Security building. Then number three, a heavy-set man in his seventies with a polyp on his intestines, broke up one of the pallets and stacked the planks in the barrel. Beneath the planks he'd already put some little branches he pulled off the mulberry tree on the corner. They lit the fire with a newspaper. It wasn't easy because the wood was damp. But when the fire finally got going, they ripped up two cardboard boxes and tossed the pieces on top of the wood. Then they all gathered around the barrel and stretched out their hands and watched silently as the flames leapt before their eyes. All except for number two, who had brought a small folding stool from home because he suffered from sciatica and couldn't stand for very long. He opened the stool and sat down with his legs crossed and looking absent-mindedly at the fire murmured in a husky voice like a chant:

In Nios where they sent me
I saw churches and windmills
and was welcomed
by a flock of fleas

The drivers on Petros Rallis Street kept slowing down to look at them. But numbers one through five didn't care. They were very cold and knew that without a fire they wouldn't last the night out there on the sidewalk. They didn't care what people thought, they had other things on their minds. They were tired and sick. They were old. They had other things on their minds.

. . .

Number three tore up a box and threw the pieces into the fire. He stirred it with a thick branch then looked at the guy sitting on the stool.

You like it, huh? he asked.

What do you mean?

For other people to work while you sit there scratching your balls.

I told you guys, I've got a problem with my back. Didn't you hear?

We've all got something. That's why we're out here tonight. Get up and help, you old shit.

Don't talk to me like that, said the man on the stool. Tough guy. Who do you think you are, ordering us around?

I know how your kind is, said number three. Lazy bums who like to have a good time. I've met plenty of you in my day. You just cover your own ass, and everyone else can go fuck themselves for all you care.

Come on, that's enough, broke in the man who'd arrived last, number five. He was the youngest, around sixty. He wore thick glasses and his teeth looked like a broken fence, crooked and with large gaps in between. He spoke with a lisp, too. Come on, stop, he said. We've got enough going on tonight, the last thing we need is a fight.

Gap-mouthed fool, number three shot back, and went to get another cardboard box.

Number two got up off his stool then sat back down and crossed his legs the other way. He lit a cigarette and blew the smoke out hard. His hands were shaking. He took his Social Security booklet out of a plastic bag and started flipping through it noisily. He muttered something to himself. Now his legs were shaking too. Then he closed the booklet and leaned over and pointed to number three who had bent down next to the dumpster and asked the others in a whisper:

Is that guy crazy?

No one spoke. They didn't even turn to look. They kept their hands stretched out in front of them and stared at the flames wondering whether there was enough wood and cardboard for the fire, if they would manage to keep the fire going until morning.

. . .

They carried their Social Security booklets and identity cards. They carried packs of tissues and keys and coins and a few bills – some in wallets, some loose in their pockets. Each carried a bottle of water, pills and capsules for his various ailments. Number five, who'd had rheumatism for years, carried a large brown envelope of x-rays. Almost all of them carried lighters or matches and extra cigarettes to help them stay awake. Two or three carried bus passes, or tickets for the trolley or metro. Number four, who was 68 years old but had thick grey hair and a thin grey mustache, carried stones in his kidneys and a small black comb in his coat pocket. Number three carried a pair of prescription glasses that he never wore in public because he was embarrassed. Four of the five carried cell phones. Number two, who had brought his folding stool from home, carried in his wallet a photograph of his son who had died the previous month in a car accident in Halkidona. Number one, who was almost blind in his right eye, carried a booklet enumerating the miracles and visions of Saint Efraim the Martyr. He read two or three pages a day, with difficulty, to gather strength or hope or to distract himself from his troubles.

They all carried years of hard work on their backs. They carried deprivations and dreams that hadn't come true. They carried the weight of the time they had spent with their wives and children. They carried compromises they had accepted, vows they had broken. They carried betrayals they had committed and others that had been committed against them. Deep inside each carried fear and stress and worry about illness and time, which came each day like a conscientious gardener to trim off a bit of their lives.

They were poor people, with debt to the banks and unpaid bills.

One of them owed money to a loan shark.

Two or three of them carried lottery tickets, scratch-offs and quick picks.

All of them carried secrets, hidden sins and things they rarely – or never – showed to anyone else.

Number one, who had glaucoma, carried a bracelet made from elephant hair that a woman had given him many years ago at the airport as she was leaving for South Africa.

Number two carried the dog tag his son wore around his neck while a conscript in the army.

Number three had carried a Kershaw knife ever since the night he'd seen two addicts beating an old man for his money down under the pedestrian bridge.

Number four carried a keychain with the keys to his family house on Aegina which he'd been forced to sell for practically nothing.

The one who'd arrived last, number five, carried the coin he'd found in the New Year's pie five or six years ago. It was the only time in his life he'd gotten the coin in his slice and for a while he carried it around for good luck. At some point the pocket of his winter coat got a hole and the coin fell into the lining and he never went to the trouble of fishing it out. By now he'd forgotten it altogether.

. . .

They carried lots of old songs, images and memories from their childhood. They carried a nostalgia for the things of the past, a nostalgia that became more and more bitter with the passing of time, and instead of filling them with joy now only made them feel older and less capable.

They carried the smells of their homes. The stale smoke from the coffee houses they frequented. The dirty air of Nikaia. The scent of bitter orange trees blooming around Easter. Sometimes they felt as if they carried the whole city inside them, avenues and streets named after forgotten homelands or the honored dead and narrow alleyways where refugee houses sat hunched in the shadow of six- or seven-story apartment buildings. Sometimes they felt as if they carried city squares with broken benches, churches and graveyards and old outdoor cinemas that had been turned into supermarkets or nightclubs.

They carried so many images and voices, of the living and of the dead.

All of them, some more than others, carried a deep hatred of politicians and doctors and the civil servants who worked at the Social Security office – for anyone they could blame for the fact that they were out here tonight like bums on the sidewalk in the freezing cold far from their homes.

Two or three carried a deep hatred of themselves, for being so small and insignificant.

One carried his hatred of god who had proven himself to be even harsher and more unjust than people.

They carried the weight of their weakness, the weight of time, of the sicknesses that ate at their bodies.

Above all they carried a silent fear and a secret longing for the day that was dawning and all the days that would dawn after that.

. . .

Every so often someone brought a cardboard box or broke a pallet and threw the pieces into the fire. Drivers slowed to look at them as they passed. Some shook their heads, others honked, either in greeting or with derision. Most of the people in the cars were young, couples or groups of men probably headed home after a night out.

The one on the stool, number two, carried a bottle of tsipouro in a plastic bag from the Galaxy Supermarket. He opened it, took a swig and held it in his mouth before swallowing. The previous week he'd sworn on his son's bones that he would never drink again. Of course he knew the oath was no good since he'd been drunk when he gave it. But now, as the tsipouro flowed through him, burning all the way down, he felt the hair on the nape of his neck rise and something cold touching his back. He shuddered.

Hey guys, he said. Guys, why don't we call the stations?

What stations?

The stations. TV. So they'll come and show everyone what a sorry state we're in. How the little guy is sitting out here suffering in the cold. Fuck Social Security and all those government ministries.

You know, it's not a bad idea. It might just –

Forget it, big guy, said number three, who was stirring the fire with a branch he'd pulled off the mulberry tree. I don't like the sound of it.

Why?

Because. I'm not going to become a spot on TV. I've got my dignity.

The man on the stool started to laugh.

Hear that, guys? The gentlemen over there's got his dignity. Why don't you tell him to pass some over to us if he's got any to spare?

The others laughed too.

Number three looked at them and then pointed his branch at the man on the stool.

Watch it, you cripple. Don't mess with me, I dance a tough dance.

Didn't we cover that ground? number five said. Enough already. Fighting isn't going to get us through the night.

Then he turned to number one, who was standing to the side reading his book, his lips moving as if he were talking to himself.

You started to say something earlier, he said. Come on over so we can all hear.

Number one closed his book and slipped it into his coat pocket and drew closer to the fire. The corneas of his eyes were white from the cataracts, the pupils almost entirely covered.

He'd seen how the others had looked at him – he'd seen lots of people looking at him like that – and for a moment he thought it was time he bought a pair of sunglasses to wear when he went out, even at night. He didn't like for people to look at him that way. He didn't want to scare people and didn't want their pity, either.

Go on already, said number three. Or do you want us to beg?

They all gathered around the barrel and stretched out their hands, very close to the flames.

. . .

I was headed home late one night from Amfiali. It was cold and foggy but I decided to walk to save myself the taxi fare. Suddenly somewhere around the water treatment plant I hear a crash and all of a sudden there's a violin lying in front of me. It really made me jump, it was a close call. If I'd been two meters further on it would have smashed me right on the head. I look up. There's a huge apartment building so tall you get dizzy just looking at it. One of the balconies has a light on. I hear some noises and a woman shrieking. Everyone else is asleep, and no one wakes up or comes out. There isn't a soul in the street, either. And the fog is so thick you can barely see a thing.

A few minutes later I see a young guy come tumbling down the front stairs of the building. He's wearing a wife-beater and he's got one of those things on his arm, what do they call them, a tattoo. Barefoot and with his hair all crazy and the kind of eyes that make your blood freeze. But I wasn't afraid.

What's going on, man? You almost killed me.

Go fuck yourself, gramps, he answers. Not angrily but like he might start crying any second.

Then he drops to his hands and knees and starts gathering up whatever he finds on the sidewalk. The instrument is in thousands of tiny pieces. The strings in one place and the wood in another, it's a total mess. But the young guy picked up every piece didn't leave a single splinter. Then he held the whole mess cut in his arms and sat down on the stairs. He was holding the violin in his arms as if it were something alive some baby or little kid. I was standing off a little ways and watching him messing with the pieces and trying to put them back together again. Look at that, I said to myself. That violin won't ever make music again. No song will ever come from its strings. That's a damned sad sight.

The violin's a beautiful instrument, said number four, the one with kidney stones. My father, may his soul rest in peace, used to cry whenever he heard the violin. He was a refugee from –

It's nothing like the accordion, though, broke in number two, shifting on his stool. There's no instrument like the accordion. I tried everything to get my son to learn to play but he wouldn't listen to me. He never listened to me. He didn't listen to any-one. That's why he.

He took a swig of tsipouro and the same shiver ran down his back again. He stood up from the stool took the comb out of his pocket and started running it through his hair, which felt hard and prickly, like thorns.

Number three struck the side of the barrel with the branch he was holding.

Will you guys shut up already? Come on, man, what happened next?

I was thinking all that, number one continued, but I didn't say a thing. I just watched him stroking that violin and didn't let out a peep not a word as if I were a priest who'd just given a dying person his last rights. On the one hand I felt sorry for him and on the other I didn't want to say something he might take the wrong way. Because he was clearly pretty upset.

Hold on a sec, broke in number three. I missed something. Now someone's dying?

Number two, the one with the tsipouro, started to say something but thought better of it and bowed his head.

What's he laughing at? Didn't I tell you not to get on my nerves? Didn't I tell you —

We all heard you just fine, said number two. You dance a tough dance. So why don't you show us your moves? You're all talk. Come on, let's see what you've got!

Number one touched him on the shoulder. Please, he said. In the light from the fire his eyes were a strange yellow color.

Number two shuddered. He hunched over on his stool and fell silent.

Then number one turned to number three.

When a priest goes to give a dying person his last rights he's not supposed to talk, he explained. Not before and not after. Otherwise it doesn't work. I didn't know either. I found out when my Maria died. I called the priest from the hospital and he came and left without saying a word. I'd been in the hospital for a week from morning until night and hadn't shut my eyes once. I begged him to say something to me just a few words it didn't matter what. Aren't there moments in your life when you need to hear something? Moments in your life when you really need some human conversation. When you need to hear something so as not to.

He stopped and took a gulp of breath as if he were drowning. By now he was yellow all over. No one said a word. All you could hear was the roar of the fire and the wood crackling in the barrel.

Then what happened? asked number five. You didn't finish the story. What happened next?

I hear a voice overhead. I look up and see the top half of a woman hanging over the balcony railing and she's shouting and shouting. You wouldn't believe the things that came out of her mouth. I couldn't see her face or anything but she had long black hair that was hanging loose in the air. It felt like you could reach out a hand and touch it. The things that hair reminded me of. At any rate. She was cursing up a storm, a real sailor's mouth, you wouldn't believe the things she said. My jaw dropped, I'd never heard a woman cursing like that. And the young guy turns to me and says:

You hear that, gramps? It's not enough that she killed my violin, now she's swearing at me, too. But you should stick around for the next episode. I'm going to go back up there and throw her TV off the balcony. First it was her turn and now it's mine. Aren't I right? Don't worry, I'll even things up. Stick around and you'll see what kind of party we're going to throw here tonight.

That's what he said but he didn't budge at all. He just sat there and messed with his violin stretching the strings and trying to piece together the broken pieces of wood. But it was no use.

The nail on one of his toes was black.

You're going to lose that nail, I say to him. It hurts a lot to have a toenail fall off.

I don't know what got into me next, but I turned to him and said: Don't give up, kid. You've got to have hope. If you fall down you have to pick yourself right back up again.

Okay, old man, he said. Whatever you say.

And he actually stood up with the violin in his arms and started to walk away. At the door to the building he stopped and said to me:

You want to hear something I read once, gramps? It's not the fall that kills us but the sudden stop at the end. You get it? It's the sudden stop that kills us.

I thought about it for a minute.

That's a big thing you said, I finally tell him.

But he was already gone. I turned and saw him climbing the stairs inside the building with his head bent and then I couldn't see him anymore.

I walked as far as the corner and waited. I can't tell you how anxious I was. I kept thinking he was going to come out onto the balcony cradling the television and toss it into the street and then who knows what might happen with that woman. Because I was worried about her, too, even after all the curses she'd dumped down on him. I was thinking how young they were. Such young people, just kids, so where does all that hatred come from?

Then what happened? asked number three, who had practically put out the fire from stirring it so much. What happened next? Did he throw the stupid TV over the edge? Maybe he pushed his lady friend, too? She deserved it, that's for sure.

Nothing happened, said number one. I waited there for a while but nothing happened. I didn't even hear the woman's voice again. Then I saw the light go out on the balcony and everything got quiet.

What kind of bullshit is this? number three shouted, hitting the barrel with the branch again. Come on, tell us what happened next. He can't have done nothing. No way. What kind of man is he?

Yeah, he must have done something, said number five, who'd taken off his glasses and was cleaning them with his scarf. He can't have just left it at that.

Nothing happened, I'm telling you. I waited there in the fog for about ten minutes and smoked a cigarette but nothing happened. Then I left but I didn't go straight home. I was so shaken up that I couldn't sit still. So I started walking down toward the port. On the way I thought about what the young guy had said about falling and the sudden stop. I had lots of ready answers in my head but none of them suited the situation. As I walked I watched the lights down at the port grow in the mist. At first they were beautiful. Then they got frightening.

. . .

A car with a broken exhaust pipe passed by on the street. The clattering startled them all.

Go fuck yourself, you asshole! shouted number three.

Then he turned to the man with the tsipouro.

Is that how things work in your village? Yiannis treats and Yiannis drinks? Pass that bottle around, you pig.

He grabbed the bottle and poured some tsipouro into his mouth without letting the rim of the bottle touch his lips. Then he handed it to the next guy. They each took a swig.

We could have done without that story, the man on the stool said to number one. What were you thinking? You crushed our morale, goddamn it.

Yeah, said number four. He's right. He looked number one in the eye then looked away again. You crushed our morale. A real man would have done something. Instead of sitting there and whining over his broken violin. You didn't handle the whole thing very well, either. You should've given him better advice.

Number one looked at each of them in turn but didn't speak.

Number three stirred the fire with his branch and then threw it in the barrel.

Man, if I'd been there I'd have known what to do, he said. But what do you expect. The world is full of fairies these days. There aren't many men left with real dicks between their legs.

He pulled a switchblade out of his pocket and weighed it in his palm. He pressed a button and the blade sprang up, glinting in the firelight.

I know what I'd have done, he said.

Number one silently looked at each of the others with his milky eyes. He'd shrunk beside the barrel with his hands wrapped around his upper arms hiding his face in the collar of his coat. His shoulders were shaking.

What kind of people are you, he finally said.

For a while no one spoke. In the glow from the fire their faces seemed transformed, full of shadows that kept changing shape. Then someone, number three, took a step backward and tilted his head so that he was looking straight at the sky. It was gray and blurry like a TV screen with no signal. He looked at the sky with such concentration, almost motionless, as if he were trying to figure out how much the sky weighed or to calculate the distance between himself and the sky, which seemed to have sunk down so low that it was resting on the rooftops of the buildings.

This night just won't end, he said. What time is it, anyway?

And then he said:

These days I keep on dreaming that I'm falling. That I'm tripping on something and falling. I wake up in terror and my heart is pounding so hard I feel like it might burst or come flying out my ears or something. It's a terrible thing to be falling. Really. Terrible.

Now the others were looking up, too. They had all tilted their heads back and were staring up at the sky.

What's worse, though? asked number one. An endless fall or a sudden stop?

You tell us. You seem to be the reader here.

I don't know. The things I read don't agree with the things I see. Or with the things I think. Nothing agrees with anything.

The fire went out. Someone went to get another pallet. It was the second to last. And there weren't many boxes left, either.

They all huddled around the barrel. Even number two, who could feel a deep pain shooting up from his heels to the middle of his back, got up from his stool and stood with the others. They all crowded together with their hands stretched close to the fire. Very close to the fire. Their bodies were touching, their elbows and arms. They jostled and pushed against one another as if they wanted to work through their heavy winter clothing and touch one another's skin. They came as close to one another as they could get. But instead of warmth they felt a shiver pass from one body to the next – they felt a cold current leaping unrestrained and breaking the circle of bodies, heedless of the fire burning so close to them, so close to their hands so close to their chests and faces.

. . .

Early in the morning, passing by on my way to work, I found them still standing in a circle around the barrel. By then others had come and were waiting on the sidewalk, old men, women, foreigners. But they were still gathered around the barrel, those five men with faces white from cold and exhaustion, watching silently as the fire slowly died in the freezing light of day.

Charcoal Mustache

IN MARCH during one of the blackouts Takis Vassalos and I are sitting at the Existence Ouzeri on the corner of American Ladies and Bythinia Streets across from a tiny triangle they call Plateia Irinis, Peace Square, which has a strange billboard in one corner advertising Immortal Cabinets and a statue in the middle of the American doctor Esther Lovejoy who apparently saved lots of lives in these parts after the population exchange of 1922.

Takis waits tables here every evening from five to midnight, five to one, five to whenever. During the day he works as a contract laborer for the municipality. He works two jobs because he has two kids. His wife Vasso died forty-nine days ago. She was driving down to Faliro and had a heart attack in the car and some stranger saw the whole thing and brought her to Metropolitan Hospital – she was still alive and fighting, wouldn't give up – and that's where the trouble started because it's a private hospital and they refused to admit her if the guy didn't pay and of course he objected – he was just some stranger passing by,

153

what an absurd thing for them to expect of him – and while they were haggling Vasso died right there in that hospital corridor among strangers, far from Takis and her children and Takis says if he were a real man if he had a drop of self-respect he would go to that hospital with a grenade in each hand and blow the whole whorehouse sky high and take everyone with him, doctors nurses hospital directors, all those motherfuckers and a few more for good measure. If he were a real man if he still had integrity if he didn't have two kids and debts to the banks and a mortgage on his house. If this if that my whole life these days is one big if, Takis says. How did they manage to convince me that I'm weak and washed up and can't do anything anymore can't react in some way – I don't care about the money, Takis says, I don't want money or revenge. What I care about is that there's this huge injustice and I know I have to do something about it but at the same time I'm not sure who's innocent and who's guilty, if I knew then maybe things would be different, says Takis. See what I mean? Another if. If and if and if would make even a dissident diffident.

That's the kind of thing Takis has been saying recently. But tonight is different. Tonight as we sit by the window in the dark and outside it's like wartime like the occupation with darkness all around and the streets deserted and your heart freezing from the cold and dark – tonight Takis says other things. A little while ago he got up and found a gas lamp and lit it and made his boss go home – a blonde from Smyrna who's not all there in the head and who's crazy about the singer Stelios Kazantzidis and pronounces all kinds of words as if she were still back in Turkey, like köftes for keftes – and then came back to the table and looked at the strange sign in the square and asked me:

What kind of tsipouro do you want? With anise or without?

There's no wine?

Of course there is.

What are you drinking?

Tsipouro.

With anise or without?

Without.

Pour me one too.

He brings over the bottle and some smoked herring and olives and a monkfish tail and some boiled nettles then sits and picks up right where he left off. He talks about the old days. He talks about how things used to be around here for the refugees who came over in in those stinking boats in '22 and had their heads smeared with tar and how they built their first huts out of mud and had to dig wells for water and then he talks about the years after that when things got a bit better, about the peddlers who used to wander through the streets – the vegetable guys selling cucumbers and purslane, the fishmongers who brought tiny smelt from Faliro and jars of tuna or pickled fish, and the guys selling salep who crushed ice in the summer and mixed it with sour cherry juice and made something they called karsabats which you drank and felt lighter somehow and for a little while you could forget your troubles.

Takis is drinking tsipouro and staring at the advertisement in the square which keeps getting lit up for an instant by the headlights of cars coming down Kondyli and then is plunged into darkness again. He drinks some tsipouro and takes a bite of herring and talks about the old times when thousands of wild poppies used to grow here in spring and the women would gather the seeds from the poppies and knead them into bread and rusks and the boys would pick the poppies and close one hand around the big red flowers and slap it hard with the other so the poppies would burst and the petals would fly out with a paf! and their hands would turn red as if they had killed some living thing with a heart and blood and on Good Thursday the girls would gather poppies for the bier because everyone knows a poppy sprouted from the ground in front of the cross at Golgotha and it was Christ's blood dripping from above that gave the poppy its red – that's what Takis says clapping his hands to show me the sound it used to make when the kids popped the petals and then he talks about the war and the occupation and the famine and how many people died here of hunger during the occupation women and children and old people.

Like right there across the street, he says. Back then there was a well in the square and one night a girl fell in and died, dizzy from hunger or desperation, who knows. They say if you passed by at night you could hear her crying in the well and shouting for help. But now there's nothing to fear. Now that they've put asphalt over everything the roads and the squares those days are over the dead with the dead and the living with the living. Later on in '42 they had food lines here and a little girl came one day dressed in boy's clothing with a charcoal mustache on her face, she'd drawn herself a little mustache and people saw it and wondered. And when they asked about it she told them her mother had died of hunger and her grandmother too and all the girls in her family had died of hunger and that's why she'd dressed as a boy, you see, in order to trick death – he'll think I'm a boy she said and he'll let me live. For god's sake, that's what she said. Just a little girl no more than seven or eight. You see what I mean? She'd drawn herself a tiny little mustache out of charcoal. And put on boy's clothes. To trick death.

Then Takis falls silent and looks out the window again at the sign on the square that says *Immortal Cabinets Out of Aluminum and Galvanized Steel 100% Guaranteed 14 Maditou Street Across from MICROLAND* and he takes a sip of his tsipouro and swallows slowly and doesn't say anything for a while. But I feel a strange agitation. I feel like I'm hearing everything not with my ears but with my heart. The sounds hit me in the chest. Takis's voice and the hum of cars coming down Kondyli and the wind whistling through cracks around the windowpanes. I feel like my heart can hear the slow burn of our cigarettes and the click clack of the zippo and the hushed roar of the gas lamp on the table. Tonight I'm strangely agitated and I'm hearing everything not with my ears but with my heart. And I wonder if it's a bad sign, if maybe I've started to lose my mind and it worries me because everyone knows – rich and poor – that to get by in times like these your heart has to be even deafer than your ears. Everyone says it, rich people and poor people alike.

Takis wipes his hands then takes out his tobacco and rolls a cigarette with one hand on his knee and lights it and looks outside.

Immortal cabinets, he says. What do you make of that?

An empty bus comes barreling down Kondyli. The sign appears for a moment, then falls into darkness.

She was seven or eight, Takis says and blows the smoke to the side. A little girl, see. She didn't want to die, so she tried to trick death.

. . .

It's a Saturday night but the place is empty. Outside it's pitch black, just a few cars in the streets and even fewer people. The light from the gas lamp forms a hazy pale blue halo around the table and around Takis and me and fills the walls with strange shadows.

We look outside.

An old lady with a flashlight goes by. Then a girl on a bicycle. A bony pregnant dog, her belly dragging on the pavement.

It makes me afraid to see the world so dark, as if it were wartime or an occupation as if something terrible has happened. Then, for an instant, the fear becomes a kind of quietness when I think how outside it's dark and cold but I'm inside where it's warm, I'm protected, with light and food and tsipouro, and with Takis talking and talking and talking and that seems to me like the biggest comfort of all – a voice in the half-dark, a calm familiar voice, the voice of my friend, husky and sad.

I want to ask how he knows all this. How he knows what happened here in the old days, about the wells and refugees and food lines and sour cherries and poppies. How he knows that there was once a little girl who dressed as a boy and drew a charcoal mustache on her face to trick death. I want to ask how he knows all this, since he's an islander, from Amorgos, and only came to live here when he met Lena. How do you know all that, I want to ask. Is it true or are you maybe just spinning yarns? But I don't ask, I don't say a thing, I just stare out at the dark street and that strange sign in the square and I stare at the pale blue halo from the gas lamp and the shadows trembling on the walls, unrecognizable shadows that don't look like ours but like the shadows of dead people, ghosts that in tonight's darkness dared to come back up into the world and sneak in here, into the Existence Ouzeri on the corner of American Ladies and Bythinia Streets across from a tiny drop of a triangle they call Peace Square, and sit down to hear what the living have to say for themselves these days to see what they're eating and drinking. To take comfort. Or maybe to find out if the living still remember them or if they've been forgotten entirely.

Takis lights a cigarette and the click clack of the zippo hits me hard in the chest. He twirls his cigarette on the lip of the ashtray, takes a sip of his drink and looks out again at the sign in the square.

The other day, he says, this guy Vayios came in, a truck driver and a real character. He had a German guy with him, his sister's husband who didn't look German at all, a tiny little guy small and crooked. His name was Christian or Christen or something like that. He was an electrician in a construction company and last year or the year before he took a real bad fall at some building site and got hurt. For a whole year he was in and out of hospitals he'd broken every bone in his body. But he seemed like a good guy real friendly and was in a mood to treat. The place was packed and they sat down and struck up a conversation with some of the others and the German wanted to know how we're getting by these days and the others told him friend, you've never seen poverty like this before, the rich making the poor work themselves to the bone so they won't fall into poverty themselves – that's the fine kind of conversation they struck up and if one of the younger guys hadn't spoken some English it would've been tough since because the German didn't speak Greek and even with the young guy translating I'm not sure you could really call it communication. At any rate at some point the conversation turned to those old times during the war and the occupation and everyone had a story to tell and they almost drove the guy nuts. The Germans this and the Germans that and all the people those animals killed during the occupation and this that and the other thing until at some point things started to heat up and I went over and said come on guys leave the man alone you're ganging up on him and that's no way to be. And Vayios says that's right you cowards talking a big talk about resistance – and then he turns to me and says hey Takis bring some tsipouro for my brother-in-law so he can see what it's like, all they drink where he's from is beer and schnapps or schnoops whatever the fuck it's called. So I bring over some tsipouro so he'll see the kind of fire it lights in your gut. And I fill his glass and Vayios says to water it down a little because he's never had it before and who knows what might happen so I go to toss a few ice cubes into his glass but the German guy says nein nein so we say cheers and clink glasses and the poor guy tips it all back at once without even taking a breath. And he freezes in place and starts to swell up and turn bright red and his eyes are full of tears and he jumps to his feet and starts limping between the tables and shouting ai ai ai limping up and down as fast as he can as if we'd lit him on fire pointing at the tsipouro and barking ai ai ai and we're all staring at him with no idea what to do and then he pulls a comb out of his back pocket and starts combing his hair frantically like a madman, you see he thought all the hair on his head was sticking straight up from the fire in his gut so now he's pacing all around pointing at the tsipouro and combing his hair and yelling ai ai ai. I can't tell you what a scene it was. Such a scene, I can't even describe it. Everyone in the place was screaming with laughter rolling around on the floor even Vayios was laughing so what could the poor German guy do except say all his haften houften and comb his hair until he was practically bald, you should have been there to see how hard we laughed that night. And he did too. I hadn't laughed like that in years.

He stops talking and stubs out his cigarette then immediately starts rolling another. In the light of the lamp his fingers look blue. Strange fingers for a person who works as much as he does – narrow and smooth with a blueish tinge. On the ring finger of his right hand the two platinum wedding bands shine in the blue light of the lamp, like two links of a broken chain.

He lights the cigarette and tilts his head back to exhale and then continues:

At some point one guy who's a little drunk stands up and turns on the cassette player and moves the tables aside and starts to dance. When the German sees him he stands up too

162

and bows to us all and takes off his shoes and joins the other guy with a dance of his own. If you can call it dancing when the poor guy's just taking these tiny slow steps like a migrant crossing a minefield. I mean he was barely moving his legs. And the others start clapping and shouting opa opa and tossing balled-up paper napkins at him. So Vayios jumps to his feet and says cut it out you jerks don't you dare make fun of my brother-in-law the guy has so many pins in him he's like a Playmobil toy. Cut it out guys I mean it. And he goes over to try and pull the German back to his seat but the poor guy has no idea what's happening. He's got his eyes closed and his arms stretched out and he's moving in slow circles with his shoes off like he's in seventh heaven. You should have been there to see. How that broken man danced. What did he know about bouzoukis and aman amans? If Vayios hadn't been there to put a stop to it he might have danced a tsifteteli. It'll go down in the history of this place, that German guy dancing. And when they finally left Vayios had to carry him out because he was too drunk to walk. We all went to the door to watch them leave. Vayios a beast two meters tall carrying his brother-in-law in his arms like a little kid. And him looking at us and smiling and waving and talking in his language. You should have seen him. How he danced. Sweating and trying so hard to move his arms and legs. Like a little kid just learning how to control his body. It had been years since I'd seen a man so, how can I say it. At peace. That's it. At peace. I'd forgotten what it's like. The next day Vayios came back to get his brother-in-law's shoes. Things had gotten so crazy he'd forgotten them here.

Takis remembers what happened that night and starts laughing again laughing loudly and happily and in the dim artificial light of the lamp I see his mouth take on an odd shape and the wrinkles at the corners of his eyes look like prints left by small birds on wet earth, so many tiny wrinkles, like carved lines, like the prints of birds that took fright at something and rose up into the air.

I fill our glasses, we drink.

We look outside.

Our faces shine in the window like fingerprints from some enormous hand. Unrecognizable faces, the faces of people who aren't us.

Immortal cabinets.

There that still is, Takis says and blinks. Then he raises a hand to his hair and starts to smooth it with quick sudden movements as if something awful just passed through his mind or in front of his eyes as he stares out at the darkened sign in the square.

Did you know there are cabinets that never die? Everything dies except not cabinets anymore. The world is changing. Who knows if one day. You never know. Of course you'll say who's going to live long enough to see it happen. But I think about it. It's been forty-nine days, you know? And I think of the kids. The older one is obsessed with computer games. Day and night at the computer. When's he going to live when's he going to fall in love? Sure, it's technology, progress, I know. But I look at him and all I can think of is the past. I look at my son and instead of looking ahead I turn back to the past. And I feel a kind of shame as if nostalgia has become some kind of crime. And I keep dreaming of the past. I dream of how it would be if things had happened some other way. But that's a kind of madness, isn't it? You're supposed to dream about the future, not the past, aren't I right? But I can't. I can't anymore, I'm telling you, I can't. Forty-nine days. And then there's work. Day and night I see people crushed by their jobs. People who are tired and scared. As if it's no longer possible to work without being afraid. And I tell myself. I tell myself I don't want to be like that I want to fight it and not let it bring me down. But how long can you stand it. And the more time passes and the more I move forward the more my heart and mind return to the things of the past. And I think about how one day all three of us will be gone, me and my heart and my mind, too. One day I'll lose my heart and my mind and then what'll happen. I don't know what'll happen. One day. Just like that.

Outside the darkness grows, the streets are empty, the windows moan in the wind.

He pushes his chair back and lights another cigarette. His

face is lit for a moment by the flame of his lighter and then sinks back into darkness.

We look outside.

Immortal cabinets, Takis says and his voice seems to darken, too.

The light from the lamp is dimmer now, and there are no more shadows on the wall. In here, too, the darkness is spreading.

Immortal cabinets, he says.

Immortal cabinets.

Foreign. Exotic.

At night he talks a lot to Lena. Vassilis. At night Vassilis talks a lot to Lena. Some things he says to put her to sleep and others he says to keep her awake. He doesn't talk about the past, about the house that was lost or the job that was lost or the life that was lost. He talks about other things. Things far from them, foreign, exotic. The tallest buildings in the world and where they're located. Which cities will be the largest in the world in the year 2050. What kinds of animals are native to Australia. The names of volcanoes in Alaska and Indonesia. Those are the kinds of things Vassilis tells Lena at night. Foreign. Exotic.

In the beginning, when they first moved to Nikaia, he would read her fairytales. Lots of fairytales, whole collections of them. From Crete, Thessaly, Epirus, Asia Minor. All kinds of fairytales. Goblins and trolls. The man in the moon. The tree of snakes. Misokolakis the half-made man. Dakris the man born of tears. The plane tree and the forty dragons. The boy raised by bears. Alimonos and the golden branches. The man made of wheat – his favorite. Fairytales from China, India, and South America, too. All kinds of fairytales. Two or three each night all night. All the fairytales he hadn't read as a child he read to Lena on those nights. The stories helped them both. It helped them forgot their troubles for a while. Night can be a torture in troubled times. During the day things are clear, you know what to be afraid of. Work, bills, phone calls from the bank about overdue payments. But night is different. Night gets into your head. Even memories are frightening at night. They creep through the sheets like snakes. That's how memories come in the small hours. And so they turned to fairytales. Vassilis read, Lena listened. Two or three fairytales each night all night until daylight came, until the balcony door shone with the gray light of day.

Later on they agreed to stop.

It's not fair, Lena said. You always fall asleep before me.

. . .

On average we dream 1,460 dreams per year.

Each dream lasts an average of two to three seconds.

It's impossible for human beings to lick their own elbows.

The human body contains enough iron to make a small nail.

The length of your thumb is equal to the length of your nose.

A woman's heart beats faster than a man's.

At an international conference on longevity in Melbourne,

Australian professor of alternative medicine Mark Cohen announced that the rabbits he and his team pet every day at the lab live sixty percent longer than the rabbits they don't pet.

Someone in the audience asked if the rabbits were real or Playboy bunnies.

November. Tonight it turned cold and a wind picked up. Vassilis slips a hand under the covers and touches Lena's chest and rests his other hand against his own chest and tries to count their heartbeats. He counts the beats and counts the streetlights on the road across the way that he can see through the balcony door. It's a road that slopes uphill full of curves which at night seems to vanish into the sky. Vassilis doesn't know where that road goes. Sky Street – that's what he calls it. Sky Street. He keeps saying they should go there one evening in the car to see where it starts and where it ends and count the yellow streetlights from up close but Lena says no. She doesn't care what road it is or what it's called or where it starts or where it ends. She doesn't care about anything in Nikaia. We're just passing through here, she tells Vassilis. We're strangers here, passing through. Besides, it's not much of a view, she says. No mountains or trees or sea. It's all apartment buildings and utility poles. Not much of a view. I pity the people who live here. But for us it's fine. We're just passing through. Isn't that right? Tell me, I need to hear it. Tell me we're just passing through.

He slowly pulls his hand away from Lena's chest and slowly

sits up and looks outside. Two eucalyptus trees on the street below, branches joining and parting as the wind blows. Eucalyptus trees. Not native to this place but they still put down roots. Every night he looks at the trees and counts the lights on the street that seems to vanish into the sky. And every night he loses track but he never gives up. That's how Vassilis spends his nights. Counting lights, looking at trees, talking to Lena — to put her to sleep or to keep her awake. And in the morning at work the others see that he's white as a sheet from lack of sleep and they laugh.

What's up, Bill? Were you screwing Snow White again last night?

Lena lifts her head and looks at him.

Are you counting streetlights again? she asks. I don't like that street, I told you. The way it ends so abruptly. We're never going there, understand? Never.

. . .

Strange how things sometimes turn out. You grow up and experience things and read books and get to know people and places and arrive at an age that you used to believe in, and in the end it seems that everything in life is a matter of luck, that your life and everyone's life is a small inside-out universe through which everything moves blindly and without purpose, a universe without a god, without rules, without purpose – chaos. And then something happens to shake that belief and you start to wonder whether you might have made a mistake, if there might in fact be something that gives meaning to the chaos, if there might be some secret thread that ties everything in your life together, a secret thread that ties your life to the lives of others. And you get scared. You get scared because while it might be truly frightening to live in chaos it's twice as frightening to know that you live not in chaos but in a world with laws and rules that you yourself will never learn, that you're incapable of learning—no matter how hard you try, you'll never find that thin secret thread, never grasp it, never find the thing that has both beginning and end.

When the house burned down Lena was twelve weeks pregnant.

No one ever knew if the stars were to blame for what happened, if it was the solar eclipse in June or Pluto which had been ascending since April. Lena's sister had won three hundred thousand euros in the lotto and decided to give up the bookstore and live her life, travel to improbable places – Alaska, Kenya, Peru. She'd always believed that there are two ways for a person to learn about herself and the world: by reading and by traveling. Books and travel. After twenty years of books now she had the opportunity to travel wherever she wanted, to get to know people, places, smells, tastes. Wasn't it incredible? She was crazy with joy. She was almost ready to believe that there is a god after all even if she would never admit it to anyone but them – her friends would make fun of her for sure. They would get mad at her, the way they did once when she said that if we call god a human creation then whoever turns against god is turning against people, too – which must mean that atheists are all misanthropes? She'd only told her sister and Vassilis. There might be a god after all, she said. She told them she wanted them to take over the bookstore and move into her house which was next to the bookstore and look after it too. They wouldn't have to pay a cent, not even the bills.

It's a win-win deal, she said. You'll have a free house and I'll have free caretakers. So no ifs ands or buts. That's how it's going to be.

She grabbed Lena's hand and squeezed it in hers. Her mouth was trembling. She had tears in her eyes.

You guys know how to run the store, she said. And if you need anything you can always call. We'll talk every day on the phone, okay?

It was evening, near the end of May. They were sitting in the kitchen. Vassilis had made coffee for the women and was drinking cognac out of a snifter. It was getting dark but they didn't turn on any lights. Lena was toying with the beads of her necklace and looking at Vassilis.

I don't know, Vassilis said. It's all pretty sudden. I mean, it seems like a lot of responsibility. We're not cut out to be bosses. Or caretakers.

Oh, come on, said Lena's sister. Over here. Look at me. Here. I'm handing over the best bookstore in Chania and I have no doubt you'll turn it into the best bookstore in all of Crete. I'm sure of it.

She leaned over and stroked Lena's belly.

You have to consider the future, she said. It's not just the two of you anymore.

Then she opened her purse and pulled out three little boxes and opened them and showed Lena and Vassilis the three platinum crosses she'd bought – one for each of them. And for my godchild I'll get a cross with diamonds on it, she said and stroked Lena's belly again.

She held out a hand to each of them.

Everything's going to be fine, she said. I'm sure you'll manage. Have faith. That's the most important thing. People who don't believe in anything are just as unhappy as those who are searching for something to believe in. Faith isn't a road. Faith is the end of the road. Or maybe it's a road with no beginning or end. At any rate, I for one am very optimistic. Agreed?

Okay, Lena said.

If I won the lottery I'd be optimistic too, Vassilis wanted to say, but he kept his mouth shut.

173

He emptied his glass and then wiped his hand on his shirt and took his sister-in-law's outstretched hand.

. . .

When the house burned down Lena was twelve weeks pregnant.

It was the last weekend of July. Her sister had just gotten back to Athens from Mexico and was leaving again on Monday for some godforsaken place – Nepal or India or somewhere like that. Utterly insane. She wanted to buy Lena a ticket to come see her in Athens. They had to see one another, she'd missed Lena so much. And she had so many things to tell her, incredible things that she'd seen and heard in Peru and Mexico. She wanted to tell her all about the Mayans and Incas and Aztecs, the Yucatan peninsula, about the sun of Mazatlan that turns an indescribable green when it sets.

I've heard that, said Vassilis. The sun is green over there. The horses, too.

So, what do you think? Lena asked. Should I go?

Go. And make sure to talk straight with her. Ask where all this is leading. You and I are stuck here running someone else's store and living in someone else's house. Great, so she won a bunch of money and wants to play Phileas Fogg. But what about us? Our whole lives are on hold. Who knows, she might get some crazy idea in her head in the next place she goes and hand all her money over to the children of Calcutta and then disappear into the jungle to feed elephants. I have no idea. How long is this whole story going to last. I can't sleep at night. It's all I can think about.

Why? I mean, what were we before? Lena said. Weren't our lives on hold before?

She opened the fridge and poured a glass of water and set the bottle on the table. On the television they were saying the heat wave would last until Monday. Forty or even forty-one degrees. It was even worse at night, it never cooled off. She came and sat on Vassilis's lap and pressed his head against her chest. Her breasts were fuller these days and her face was puffy and glistened as if she were sweating all the time. In the mornings she felt dizzy and she was always complaining that she was tired. There were days when she didn't get to the bookstore until afternoon and didn't really help much at all. She just sat at the register and read baby books.

It's not like we're strangers, Lena said. She's my sister. It's not just anyone's store and house. What's gotten into you?

But they're not ours, either. They're not a stranger's but they're not ours, either. The uncertainty is driving me nuts.

He took a cigarette out of the pack and put it in his mouth without lighting it. For the past month or so Lena hadn't let him smoke in the house. She was trying to get him to quit. And drinking, too. Things were different now, she said. The days are over when you could play Billy the Kid. You're going to be a father soon, she said and laughed. You're going to be Kyrios Vassilis. And then Kyr Vassilis. And then barba-Vassilis. And I'll be Aunt Lena.

And she laughed.

He toyed with the cigarette in his fingers then laid it down on the table. Lena drank her glass of water one mouthful at a time. She held it in her mouth until it got warm and then swallowed slowly. The way he was looking at her sideways, and the way her neck was bent, her face seemed unrecognizable to him. Distorted. He closed his eyes.

It's not fair, he said.

What?

The whole thing. Three hundred thousand. Three hundred thousand. I can't wrap my head around it. And she never said, hey, guys, here's a couple grand for you to go and spend however you like. All she gave us were those stupid crosses. As if we're Mau Mau or something. That's one nice sister you've got. You should be proud.

Lena stood up from his lap and sat on a different chair. She looked at the bottle of water sweating on the table.

Pity the man with no nails who expects others to scratch his back, she said. That's what my mother used to say.

Then she said she was scared to fly with the baby. She'd talked to her doctor and he said it was fine. But she was still scared.

Go, Vassilis said. Go and talk to her. Explain how things are over here. Tell her that something has to give.

I'll go. But I'm scared.

All of a sudden her upper arm was covered in tiny little bumps. She set her glass on the table and started to rub her skin.

I'm fine, she said. It's okay. It's gone now.

Then they fell silent. They stared at the sweating bottle of water on the table. A drop rolled down from the neck of the bottle. Then another. And another.

. . .

An entire weekend. He couldn't remember how long it had been since he'd had the house to himself for an entire weekend. Years and years. In the morning he drove Lena to the airport and on the way home he started quaking all over with nostalgia. Nostalgia for the years before he was married, when he drank alone, walked alone for hours from Pahiana to Souda and back again. Alone. With other worries, or no worries at all. Alone.

He opened the bookstore and before noon had talked to Lena on the phone once or twice and emptied an entire bottle of tsikoudia. Then he went next door to the house and kept drinking and put on music and started to dance in the darkened living room and as he danced and sweated and drank he remembered the years when music was his only friend, the years when music

177

gave him strength and made him feel invincible. He remembered the years when he dreamed of becoming a singer, a rock star, giving concerts and interviews. New Idols, that's what his band would be called.

From Nietzche's Zarathustra and it meant something but he'd forgotten what.

Soon he got tired and dizzy and he lay down on the floor to catch his breath. In life you don't get what you deserve but what you demand, is what the self-help books say. And there, in the darkness, looking at the things around him that weren't his, smelling the strange smell of the house, it occurred to him that he'd never demanded anything in his life. And he realized that now, even if he wanted to, it was far too late to demand anything at all.

He remembered something that had happened the previous October when they were still living in their old place. It was Sunday evening, outside it was rainy and windy. He was lying on the sofa and listening to the rain and feeling the spot on his chest where the doctor had shaved off a patch of his hair. The doctor had shaved him and put on some doodad with suction cups that was supposed to monitor his heart rate. On Wednesday he'd fainted at the store just like that for no reason. Lena took him straight to a cardiologist. Blood pressure meter, cardiograph, echocardiogram. The guy poked and prodded for an hour. Are you experiencing any kind of stress, he asked and

Vassilis said no but it wasn't true. They were out of money again – Lena's sister had some kind of debts and wouldn't be able to pay them until the end of the month. And they were down to their last hundred euros.

Cut back on coffee and cigarettes and alcohol, the doctor told him. And salt. And start walking. And make an appointment to come back for a stress test. I don't see anything serious but the older we get, the more the old ticker needs looking after.

The cardiologist charged seventy euros. Fifty for the office visit and twenty for the machine.

He was still listening to the rain and rubbing his chest where the doctor had shaved him when Lena bent over him and kissed him on the ear. Wake up, she said. Get up, I have a surprise for you. She took his hand and put her other hand over his eyes and pulled him into the kitchen. For a moment – who knows why – he thought that he would open his eyes and see a pile of money spread out on the kitchen counter. When he opened his eyes he saw a plate of cookies.

Ta-da! Lena cried and laughed and clapped her hands. What do you think? You're going to love them. You've never tasted cookies like this before, believe me. Don't try them yet, I'm going to make some hot cocoa first. Your little Lena sure can cook sometimes, these are real gourmet treats.

She made the hot cocoa and lit some candles and put 16 Horsepower on the stereo and opened the balcony door. They sat on the sofa and ate cookies made with grape must and drank cocoa listening to music, watching the rain and smelling the wet earth. The cookies were crunchy, with sesame and cinnamon.

There's nothing I'm afraid of right now, said Lena. She looked him in the eye. I'm not worried about work or money. Nothing. I'm not even afraid of illness. Really. I don't know why, I just have this faith inside. I believe in Christ. I believe in us. There's nothing else I need. Nothing.

He started to say something but she stopped him.

Shut up, she said, and take me to bed.

. . .

It was nighttime when Lena called. What's wrong, she asked. Why do you sound like that? He told her he'd been sleeping and she woke him up. He told her he was going back to bed and they'd talk in the morning. Then he went into the kitchen and turned on the oven to heat up his dinner. Lena had made goat with potatoes. He ate straight out of the pan like an animal, with his hands. He was hungry. He ate half the pan and drank another bottle of tsikoudia – his third that day. When he opened the fridge to take out the bottle he looked at the empty shelves and the frozen white light coming out of the fridge. The cold hit his face. He felt as if he had opened the door of some strange foreign world that was ready to suck him up. He closed the door of the fridge and held it shut with both hands.

Then he left the house.

He went down Kidonia Street and crossed over into the square and then out onto Halidon Street and headed down to the port. He turned right onto a sidestreet and ducked into a bar called Labyrinth. He hadn't been there in years. The bartender was different. The music was different. The people were different – now it was full of queers in shorts with gel in their hair. He looked at the women. They all looked pregnant. Fat and pale and sweaty. He felt like throwing up. He ran back outside. He bought cigarettes and more tsikoudia from a mini-market on the corner and headed on foot for Souda Bay. His boots slapped heavily against the pavement. He wore boots year round, winter and summer, had ever since he was in school. He liked the smell of the leather, the sound the heels made, the feeling of security on his feet. He felt as if he were wearing armor. He hated normal shoes, thought it shameful for a man to let his socks show. Though recently Lena had been pressuring him to wear sneakers in summer. You're going to mess up your feet if you don't let them breathe, she said.

Outside the schools in Koumbes he tripped over a broken sidewalk tile and almost fell. His right boot got scratched. He bent over and rubbed it with his hands, stroking the stiff black leather.

No, he said. No way. As long as I live I'll always wear boots. End of story.

And he was glad he'd finally found something to demand.

. . .

When the house burned down Lena was twelve weeks pregnant.

He didn't see anything or hear anything either. But he could smell the burn from the next street over. And when he turned the corner he saw a crowd gathered outside the house. Someone ran toward him shouting his name and grabbed him by the shoulders. He saw the door of the house which had been busted open, and the blackened walls, the street full of water. The window of the bookstore was in ruins. They made him sit down on the steps of the house across the street and brought him water. Everyone was talking at once. A fire. The oven was on. The fire department. We were looking for you. That's what he remembers. And he remembers an old woman splashing his face with water and rubbing his cheeks hard, and his forehead and neck and crying and saying oh that poor unlucky girl.

The same words, again and again.

Oh that poor unlucky girl. That poor unlucky girl. That poor unlucky girl.

. . .

Talking to Lena so she'll fall asleep or so she'll stay awake. It depends. But talking. All night every night. Until his voice in the dark of the bedroom starts to sound like it's not his voice but just a sound in the night, a sound that belongs to the night. All night every night. In the morning he steals time from work and searches the internet or flips through American almanacs in search of evidence and facts and numbers. He prepares himself as best he can for the night because at night he has to talk to Lena – he can't let her down, can't let her go hungry. Because Lena is hungry. And the night is hungry. And Vassilis feeds them both with useless things, with trivia – facts, evidence, numbers – because if he doesn't feed them they'll eat him instead. So each night he talks and talks and talks until his mouth goes dry and each day he hopes for just a single night when he can go to sleep quietly, to fall asleep just once without talking without dreams without worries.

Tonight he talks again to Lena about the mysteries of the human body and of sleep and dreams.

And then he tells her about Dr. Cohen's rabbits.

At an international conference on longevity in Melbourne, Australian professor of alternative medicine Mark Cohen announced that the rabbits he and his team pet every day at the lab live sixty percent longer than the rabbits they don't pet.

Lena stirs a little and murmurs something then stops. It must be a dream, Vassilis thinks and counts to three, since the average dream lasts between two and three seconds. But it might also be the cold. It's been almost a month that the heat's been turned off. The whole apartment building ran out of petrol, the tenants don't have money to pay the monthly fees. For the past month the tenants have all been squabbling. Apartment buildings. Cold, damp, paper-thin walls. Walls that might as well be paper. Noise from people during the day noise from things at night. Doors closing, taps running, televisions on full blast. Noise. An endless hum in the night. In the other house it was different. The other house was a house with everything a house should have. And now it's gone. But he doesn't talk about that to Lena. He doesn't say anything about the house that was lost or the job that was lost or the life that was lost.

He gets up out of bed holding his breath. Very slowly and carefully. It seems to him that it takes a whole hour to stand up from the bed. And another to walk out of the bedroom because the floor squeaks. It growls like an animal that's had its tail stepped on. From the bedroom to the kitchen is another hour.

It's like going from Chania to Souda Bay, Vassilis thinks.

In the kitchen he lights a cigarette and cracks open the window to let the smoke out. November. It's windy again tonight. And cold. He smokes and feels cold and thinks how nice it

184

would be if he had some tsikoudia tonight, a drop of wine, something. He smokes and remembers that uncle of his whose wife locked him in the house so he wouldn't go to the tavern and he sat there and drank all of her perfume. They'd fired him from his job two years before he would have been eligible for retirement. That's when things took a turn for the worse. He found work wherever he could, even delivered souvlaki on a motorbike. And no one could believe a man could become a drunk in his sixties.

He smokes and strange thoughts pass through his mind.

He smokes and looks at the eucalyptus trees on the street below, how the branches come together and part in the wind. He smokes and counts the streetlights on the street across the way that seems to vanish into the sky. Sky Street. He keeps saying they should go there one evening in the car to see where it starts and where it ends and count the yellow streetlights from up close but Lena says no.

I don't like that street, she says. The way it ends so abruptly. We're never going to go there, you understand? Never.

He smokes until the cigarette burns out all on its own and then he opens the tap in the sink just a smidge and throws his cigarette butt down the drain. He checks the burners on the electric stove one by one. He makes sure there are no candles burning, makes sure the toaster isn't plugged in, or the water heater left on. He makes sure the danger of a fire is negligible.

Lena has her hands crossed over her chest. As soon as he lies down beside her she opens her eyes.

What happened, she asks. Why did you stop?

I thought you were asleep. Sorry.

Don't stop. Talk. So I can hear your voice.

She closes her eyes. Vassilis turns over onto his side propping himself on his elbow and looks out at the lights on the street that climbs up the hill. Then he bends over Lena and starts to stroke her ears. Slowly and gently with circular motions he strokes Lena's ears. It's the first time he's ever done that. The first time. He can hear his heart beating. Lena makes a cooing sound and in the darkness he thinks he sees her lips trembling. But it could just be his imagination. Except she's definitely cooing – and it's the only sound that doesn't frighten him. The only sound in the night that pours a drop of sweetness into his heart.

And then he starts to talk again.

For Poor People

LOSING YOUR JOB is like breaking a limb.

The afternoon when they fired us I went down to the port. By foot from Korydallos like a hunted man Halkidona Maniatika then straight down Thermopyle to Agios Dionysios and the dock where the boats for Crete come in. I went like a hunted man because the day seemed frightening somehow a day in July and the place black with heat. There was a strange light that day black and harsh as if some curse had changed the shapes of things and made everything unrecognizable houses roads cars everything unrecognizable as if you were a stranger in a strange land and all the people had vanished and all you saw was a frightened dog every now and then licking the water that dripped from the air conditioners overhead that shuddered and panted and I kept walking and looking up at those air conditioners and saying up there it's another day another country a cool day in a country that sleeps cool and full and scared. I kept going but it wasn't easy it was as if something had broken inside me and I kept thinking about what Aris had said while emptying his locker and folding his uniform and gloves and the khaki work belt and all his stupid clothes he had to wear on the job folding them all slowly and carefully as if they weren't dirty stained work clothes full of holes but the clothes of some person who had suddenly died and left them all behind and someone else who was still alive had to gather them someone always has to do that someone always has to gather the things of the dead because the things the dead leave behind are the last bits of rope binding them to this world and some living person always has to untie those last bits of rope because no man is an island right we're just boats.

That's what Aris said.

Losing your job is like breaking a limb.

. . .

I had a place down at the port. A place all my own, like a second home, a rickety wooden bench over by where the trucks headed for Crete sat and waited to load. I sat there too every evening, winter and summer, for hours, and watched the ships coming in and out of the port and the people and cars and trucks embarking and disembarking. If I had anything to drink I drank and sang, always the same song, always "Sittin' On the Dock of the Bay" – Otis Redding is just the thing for someone spending his hours down at the port, at the dock, where the sea meets the land, where everything is both together and apart, where people come together or part, like sand and waves, sometimes calm and indifferent and sometimes with a terrible roar and passion. Even if I was sober I still sang the same song, always the same song, and it bothered me that I could never get Otis's whistling right, not once, not a single time, drunk or sober – I sing like a bald crow and whistle like a pelican, as Aris used to say. If the weather was nice I would stay and watch the sunset. I watched the sun and the light from the sun falling on things, the last rays before the sunlight disappeared, I watched the light from the sun slip slowly over the ships and the warehouses and over the apartment buildings that lined the port over the people drinking coffee on their balconies or smoking or watching television or driving or walking or running to catch the bus and over women hanging clothes out to dry on the tops of buildings and children hiding behind sheets which were white or printed and pretending to be ghosts and shouting boo and frightening their mothers. Over the sparrows and the turtledoves that cooed and flapped their wings and drank the water that dripped drop by drop from the solar-powered water heaters. And the things I saw were more beautiful and hurt my eyes more than what I thought I was seeing, because what I thought I was seeing was fire. A fire that burned the world from the inside, without flames or smoke, a fire that burned the world silently and secretly and punishingly. Aris didn't believe any of it, didn't believe that the birds drank water that dripped from the water heaters or that I saw fires burning without smoke or flames, but one Christmas Eve – the last Christmas I remember it snowing at the port, and when I went down and saw my bench from a distance it was buried in a pile of crusted snow and I thought it looked like a huge delicious Christmas cookie covered with powdered sugar, or like an unborn snowman waiting to come into the world, waiting for someone to turn him into a proper snowman, with a pudgy body, a round head, and a carrot for a nose – that Christmas Eve Aris bought me a present with part of his Christmas bonus and gave it to me as we were getting off work. It was wrapped in shiny red paper with Saint Vassilises and flying sleighs pulled by reindeer without antlers. When I tore the paper and opened the box I saw a pair of goggles like the kind welders wear, a big pair of goggles with orange protective plastic and very thick lenses.

He grabbed me by the shoulders, hugged me, kissed me next to my ear. He smelled of tsipouro and smoke and work. His eyes shone in the frozen light of day.

For the port, he says. For you to wear when the fires come so your eyes don't burn. How do you like them? Try them on. Aren't they great? Do you like them?

He had a firm grasp on me, wouldn't let go.

Merry Christmas. Merry Christmas, and here's to many more. Here's hoping the bad times are over.

Then he stepped back and pretended he was holding a micro-phone and looked at me and started to dance and sing.

Your fireproof eyes have shattered me
I'm shattered by your fireproof eyes

Everyone gathered around and watched us drunkenly and clapped and laughed.

That Christmas Eve at work, at a spare parts warehouse in Korydallos, amid laughter and songs with the snow outside covering the world and the world glistening white and cold and harsh as a marble threshing floor.

. . .

That's why I noticed her at first. Because her hair seemed to have caught fire and be burning without smoke or flames. After the initial shock, I put on my special goggles which I always had with me, hanging from my belt loop, and thought how she deserved to burn up entirely – though she had beautiful hair, thick and golden like a halo – she deserved to burn because she was sitting on the wooden bench, on my bench, my second home. I didn't like it. It wasn't right, wasn't how things should be. It was like coming home from work and finding a stranger with her feet up on your sofa. The way she was dressed wasn't right either. It was the middle of July and she was sitting there in an overcoat, black pants, and boots. I stopped a ways off and watched her, devoured her with my eyes. She was sitting cross-legged, wrapped in her coat, hands in her pockets, staring through half-closed eyes at the water. And through my special goggles I saw the sun reddening her hair and saw the wind mussing her hair and told myself that I was seeing a tree whose trunk had been blackened by fire and the fire was climbing higher and burning the tree's thick branches and tender leaves. And right away I gave her a name. I called her the lady with the little coat, because as everyone knows if you give a name to something foreign to you, if you name the thing that's foreign your fear of the foreign recedes. It didn't matter that she was too young to be a lady and didn't look at all like a lady or that her coat wasn't little but a regular overcoat, black and heavy, down to her knees. It's still what I called her. The lady with the little coat. Because I needed to give her some name. And because she didn't have a dog.

. . .

Losing your job is like breaking a limb.

At first you don't feel anything, Aris said, the break is still fresh and it doesn't hurt. The pain and the fear come later, when the wound cools. When you remember the rent and the bills and the help wanted ads in the paper. The phone calls each morning, the harsh voices on the other end. Sorry, someone else beat you to it. Call again tomorrow. Send us a resume and we'll see – these days they want a resume for a job moving furniture. The pain and the fear come later, Aris said. Aris, who got tossed out onto the street with me like cigarette butts without an explanation, just a phone call. Aris, who said he didn't know what he might do tonight – I might hang myself with my belt, he said, or go down to Faliro and drown myself in the sea. We'll see. I haven't decided yet. Depending on my mood. If I had a gun it would be easier. Once and for all, no messing around. The poor guy had taken it to heart, even though we both knew it was coming, we'd known for a while. It was just a matter of time, as they say. You guys in the warehouse they're going to cut your heads off svin svin svin with a laser, the jaundiced guy over in accounting had been telling us. Svin svin svin, he said to Aris whenever they ran into one another in the hall or the cafeteria. Svin svin svin – and he'd laugh. He was right, the bastard, they threw us out just like that, no laser just a phone call. They called in the morning and by noon we were out on the street. And then something strange happened. As we were leaving, Aris stopped for a drink of water from the spigot by the entrance. July, the middle of the day, incredibly hot. But when he turned on the spigot – it was one of those big garden spigots, with the nozzle turned upwards – the water jumped out at high pressure and hit him in the face and almost knocked him to the ground. I'd never seen anything like it. He jumped backwards as if he'd been shot. He stumbled, gave me this awful lost look. Soaked from head to toe, water dripping from his hair and his collar and his arms. He looked at me and didn't say a word but his eyes spoke and spoke and spoke. I'm fifty-two years old, they said. With a son in the army and a daughter at the University of Crete. And their mother working four-hour shifts at the supermarket. And credit card debt. And now you and I are out of a job. And I'm fifty-two. So what's going to happen now? What do we do now? Can you tell me that?

I went over to him, grabbed his arm, took him to the bus stop. When the bus came he got inside and our eyes met through the window. His mouth had run out of words, but his eyes said all kinds of things.

I don't know if my eyes spoke, or what they might have said to Aris.

. . .

I sat at the very edge of the dock where the cement made a corner with my legs hanging over the inky blue black dark red water with its film of petrol and bubbles and trash. I looked at the lady with the little coat. July, forty degrees in the shade and she's sitting there wrapped in her overcoat as if she were living in some other season on some other day in some other world. I looked at the ships and water and seagulls diving from up high and they looked back at me with their bloodthirsty yellow

eyes. I tried to see everything, to smell and hear everything –
the wind and the waves and people's voices and the hum of the
engines. Not to pass the time but so it wouldn't pass, because
time isn't medicine, it doesn't heal all wounds, on the contrary,
time is the worst doctor, as that Trypes song goes. I looked
at the enormous ship, the Lissos, which was about ready to
put out to sea and was swallowing people and cars and trucks
into its dark belly. I looked at the lady with the little coat who
was watching the ship and I said to myself she can't be traveling anywhere and she hasn't come here to see anyone off and
I said to myself it just isn't normal – but what else that day had
been normal? And then I saw them lowering a big hose from
the side of the ship and the water gushing out of it into the sea
and I thought about Aris again. How he'd jumped back when
the water hit him, how he'd stumbled weakly, how he looked
at me when the water slapped him in the face. And I said for
sure he wouldn't hang himself with his belt tonight or go down
to Faliro to drown himself in the sea. I said for sure he'd be
sitting on the sofa smoking and drinking tsipouro without anise
and watching television. Because he'd told me plenty of times.
If you're down or have something on your mind, he said, just
turn on the television. It's the best medicine, just take it from
me. TV. For people like us, for poor people, there is no other
medicine.

. . .

When the ship left its moorings, when the dock emptied of
port officers and passengers and cars, when the waves from the
wake stopped slapping the thick tires that lined the side of the
dock, the lady with the little coat got up off my bench and went
over to the edge of the pier and perched on a mooring bollard.
She sat with her hands in her pockets and looked at the ship
vanishing off to our right. A pale face, she hadn't spent much
time in the sun. She sat there until the ship disappeared and
the smoke from its funnel and the long foamy wrinkles ships
leave in their wake as they steam away. Then she kneeled in
front of the bollard and pulled three cans of spray paint from
her pockets and shook them vigorously and started to paint
the black metal of the bollard. It was something else to see.
Something else, really. How she moved her hands so deftly
and gracefully, switching cans, stopping to correct something
then continuing her work hunched over, silent and engrossed –
I only saw her raise her head once and look off into the distance
in the direction of where the ship had gone.

When she was done she rubbed her hands on a cloth she
pulled out of her pocket – who knows what else she was hiding
in that little coat – and then stood up tall and took two steps
back and looked at the bollard cocking her head to one side

and then went back to the bench. I waited. I waited for some time to pass trying to be discreet about it. Then I stood up and walked toward the bollard, feigning indifference, looking at the sea with my hands blocking the sun from my eyes, as if I were waiting for a ship that would take me to where I wanted to go or for a ship that would bring me someone I wanted to see. I was expecting her to have painted something really special but all I saw when I went over there was something that looked like a child's drawing. A yellow smiley face with black eyes and very red lips. It was no work of art or anything but I kept on staring at it and wondering: What was it, what did it mean? What did it mean to paint a little yellow person – it wasn't a man or a woman either – with an enormous red smile on a mooring bollard. What was it, what did it mean. The woman on the bench was also staring at the bollard – she paid no attention to me, like I wasn't even there, though I was actually standing right in front of her wearing my welding goggles with the thick lenses and orange protective plastic. She had wrapped herself in her overcoat with her hands deep in her pockets letting the breeze muss her hair which now that the sun was disappearing behind the apartment buildings had lost its shine and grown darker around the edges like a halo in an old icon. It was like coming home after work and finding a strange woman sitting on your sofa staring silently at a painting she's made on the opposite wall. And my mind went again to Aris. If he'd been there he would have gone over and talked to her for sure. For sure. He'd sit next to her and offer her a cigarette and start asking all kinds of questions and talking to her in his calm gruff voice.

Don't sit here, he would finally say. This is no place for a girl to be sitting by herself. Go home and turn on the television. It's a good thing, television. It's like medicine. It really is. The best medicine. Really.

. . .

It was getting dark. A ship came into the port and turned itself around and docked with its stern facing the pier. It was empty, no passengers or cars either. When the ramp came down a sailor came out and grabbed the rope and pulled it over to the painted bollard. For a minute he froze in place, bent over, looked at the yellow smiley face, then laughed, shook his head and laughed again and looked around but didn't see anything so he threw the rope around the bollard and went back to work.

I waited. A breeze had picked up and in the half darkness I could hear another rope slapping against the empty flagpole on the stern of the ship. I could pick out that sound in an instant from among thousands of other sounds. There's no other sound like it, so lonely and melancholy, an unending sigh, an empty flagpole longing for its flag. I'd never told Aris about it, because I knew he wouldn't believe me and also because he'd think nothing of running out to buy me a pair of ear protectors like the ones the guys wear who work the jackhammers, the ones with the spongy cushions that rest softly over your ears and make your ears all hot and he'd give them to me and say:

For the port. For you to wear when it's windy so you don't have to hear how sad the flagpole is. Aren't they nice? Try them on. Aren't they nice?

. . .

Now the wind was blowing hard. A hot harsh wind that stuck to you like old sins. I saw the girl get up off the bench and go over to the bollard. She kneeled and pulled the cans of spray paint back out of her pocket – or it might have been just one can, I don't know, I couldn't see very well. She did something to the bollard and then got up and stood there motionless and looked for a while at the dark sea and put her hands in her pockets and wrapped herself in her coat and left almost at a run with her head down. She went out through the gate, crossed the street and disappeared. When I went over to the bollard I saw that she'd changed something in the painted face. The smile. There was no smile anymore, she'd erased it. She'd erased the smiling red lips and in their place had put a black line that curled downward, a thick black line like a wound or scar. She'd erased the smile from the happy face and now the happy face was sad and afraid. At first I didn't get it. Why had she done it? That smiley face had been a kind of comfort. To sit all alone at the port at night and see a smiley face on a bollard was a kind of comfort – why would she want to ruin it? But later on, when I sat down on the bench, I looked again and understood. I saw the rope squeezing the neck of the fake person like a noose and choking it. That's why she'd erased the smile and made the happy face sad. Because it was choking. Because it had a thick rope around its neck and it couldn't breathe.

I took off my special goggles and rubbed my eyes and looked again.

It's an awful thing to have a noose around your neck. Even for a painting, for a fake person, it's an awful thing. Really.

. . .

By now it was night. Off in the distance, outside the port, the lights of the ships anchored out at sea flickered in long irregular lines like the beads of a broken necklace whose pieces had scattered in the dark. I couldn't see them from where I was sitting but I knew that's how they were. Little shiny beads scattered in the dark – and you stretched out a hand and thought you could touch them, but that necklace had broken once and for all, no one could put it back together again. I sat down on my bench. At last. I sat there like a person who's just come home exhausted from work – legs straight out eyes closed arms stretched to either side. I ran my hand over the peeling wood, which was warm and scratchy. I smelled my hand. It smelled like salt and sun and fuel oil.

Then I got up and went to the edge of the dock and kneeled in front of the bollard and touched the metal and the sad face that was painted on it. It was wild to the touch, wild and warm. I stood up and grabbed the thick wet rope with both hands. I grabbed the noose that was choking the painting's neck. I grabbed it with both hands, with all my strength, and tried to pull it off of the bollard.

I grappled with the rope and sang that same song, "Sittin' On the Dock of the Bay," the same one I sing every night, and I said to myself that tonight I might just manage to get the whistle right, Otis Redding's whistle, just once. It wasn't easy but I'd give it my best. And I'd loosen the noose. I'd loosen the noose and take the rope off the bollard so that painted fake person could breathe. Man or woman it didn't matter.

I struggled with the rope, gave it all the strength I had, told myself I had to succeed. I wished Aris were there to see what I was doing and tell me whether it was a good thing, whether it was a kind of medicine, to take ropes off bollards and loosen nooses from the necks of painted people. I wished he could tell me if that too was medicine for people like us, for poor people.

The noose was awkward and the rope kept slipping, chafing my hands until they bled.

But I wouldn't stop, I gave it my all, I tugged at the rope with all my strength.

Please, I said. Please help me.

I struggled to take off that noose. I gave it all my strength.

It was July. Saturday was dawning. The sea breathed small choppy waves.

The Union of Bodies

How much.

Four hundred.

How much?

Are you deaf? Four hundred. One hundred times four. At the end of the month.

You said eight hundred. You said you'd ask for a whole month's wages.

I said, past tense.

And you accepted four.

That asshole doesn't listen to anyone. And I begged him. Anyway. Four hundred is fine. I'm going over there now. We'll talk in the morning.

Did you try giving him a blow job?

Effie.

You should be ashamed. You call yourself a man? If you were a whore he'd give you more. I don't want to ever see you again, you hear? Don't you dare show your face around here because I'll call the cops. I'm sick of you, you pathetic fool. You're small change. It's over, we're through. Hear me? We're through. Just listen to him, four hundred. That's a euro per hour. You pathetic idiot. Loser. You'll always be someone's bitch.

. . .

The receiver is black and heavy in his hand. He hangs up and leaves the phone booth and crosses the street to get back in the Nissan. Four hundred euros. He rolls down the window and straightens the mirror and looks at himself. Four hundred euros.

He looks at himself in the mirror. He has black circles under his eyes and the whites of his eyes are full of tiny red threads. His mouth tastes like something died in there. He hasn't eaten or slept since yesterday. He smooths his hair back and runs a hand over the top of his head and can feel the shards of glass. Little pieces of glass under the skin. It's got to be glass. In May he crashed the car into a low wall around a field. Early in the morning on the fourteenth of May. He was going a hundred kilometers an hour and went straight through a wall down in Aspra Homata on Beloyannis Street. He wasn't wearing a seat belt and his head hit the windshield and the airbag even opened. He wasn't hurt, just a few scratches. But the Nissan was totaled. At the dealership they wanted ten thousand to fix it. Ten thousand euros. As much as he'd paid for it new. He felt like grabbing the bastard by the throat and strangling him. In the end he found a mechanic in Keratsini who got it back into some kind of shape for two thousand. Effie loaned him half. He still owes her for it.

And the Nissan drives like a boat these days. Every time he gets in he's worried it might not start.

He doesn't remember hitting the wall. He only remembers getting out of the car and checking to make sure nothing was broken and then walking to Effie's house and the whole way feeling his head and finding little pieces of glass. From Kokkinia to Agia Sophia by foot, who knows how he managed that. He remembers Effie opening the door and screaming and making him lie down in the bedroom. She wanted to call an ambulance but he wouldn't let her. She sat there all night by his side and talked to him. He can't remember what she said. He only remembers swearing that he'd never drink again. And ever since then whenever he breaks his oath he's afraid. Which means he's afraid when he drinks and afraid when he doesn't drink, too. Fear.

He grabs his cell phone off the dashboard and puts it in the glove compartment. The battery is dead again. For ages he's been saying he needs to get a charger for the car but he always forgets. And today the battery ran out of juice and he ran out of money. Again.

He holds his hands up in front of him so they're facing one another and stretches out his thumbs. They're trembling slightly. He holds his breath then slowly lets it out and lets his fingers relax and watches as they approach one another slowly and hesitantly until they're tangled together like lovers' bodies – his fingers coming together like lovers, like people touching in search of shelter from some terrible disaster.

He sits like that for a while with his thumbs together and thinks of all the things he needs to do, and of the nights he'll spend with Effie. Then he turns the key in the ignition and releases the emergency brake and sticks his head out the window. Somewhere someone is cooking and the air smells like french fries. He closes his eyes and takes a deep breath and sighs.

Four hundred euros. Four hundred. At the end of the month.

And it's still only the third of August.

. . .

Its name is Leben. A Belgian sheepdog with bloodthirsty eyes and jet black fur that shines even at night. He's only seen the dog three times and all three times it lunged at him, then walked off and stared at him with its mouth half open and its long pink tongue hanging out. It watched him and laughed. Fucking dog. From a distance it looked like a bear.

And Alamanos laughed too.

Don't be scared, man, he said. It's just until he gets used to you. Look at you, shitting yourself with fear.

Alamanos asked him to come by the house last week so he could give him instructions and show him where things were. There isn't another house like it in all of Schisto. People pass by and marvel. The house itself sits on five hundred square meters and has another two thousand of yard. A pool and grass and strange trees and hidden lights in the garden. A covered patio with a built-in grill and wood-fired oven. And the whole thing enclosed in a high stone wall with cement on top where they've stuck pointy pieces of sharp green glass that glitter in the sunlight so that from a distance it looks like an enormous grey dragon sunning itself on the top of the wall and looking out with a thousand shiny eyes.

It's stupid, that dragon, said Alamanos. The wife's idea. She saw it on television. You know how women are. Whatever bright idea gets stuck in their cunt.

He showed him how the alarm worked, how to turn on the lights in the house and in the garden, how to water the grass and how the lawn mower worked. He showed him which keys opened which doors and explained what to do with the dog. How and when to feed it, how often to walk it. They would be gone for all of August – ten days abroad, in Tunisia or Morocco, and the rest touring the islands on their yacht – and Alamanos needed someone he trusted to look after the house and the dog. And he said he would do it. Not just for the money but also to get on Alamanos's good side. Times are tough. Things at work aren't going well at all. A bagmaker. That's his job. He puts newspapers and magazines and flyers in plastic bags. But things have been getting messy since spring. There's no cash to speak of. Everyone's been working on credit. Alamanos has been fighting with the customers and the customers are leaving and orders are dropping like flies – and Alamanos is firing people, too. The Poles and the Russians were the first to go but starting in September there'll be others, too. For sure. So he's afraid of losing his job. He hates his job and hates having to lie about what he does. A bagmaker. When he was little and people asked him what he was going to be when he grew up he never knew what to say. But it never occurred to him, he never could have imagined that one day he'd have a job like that. Most people don't even know there is such a job. Bagmaker. They don't even know what it means. That's why when people ask what he does he just says he works in the private sector. And if they insist – the way Effie did when they first met – he says he operates packaging machines. Or works at a graphic arts firm. Bagmaker. Because if you really think about it even that's a lie. He doesn't make bags. He puts things in bags. Newspapers magazines promotional flyers. So he's not a bagmaker, he's something else. He just doesn't know what.

But he still doesn't want to lose his job. So when Alamanos mentioned the house, he offered immediately. It's good to be on good terms with the boss. It's good for your boss to trust you

208

and be indebted to you in some way. It's a great opportunity. A man doesn't entrust his house and his property to a nobody. An operator of packaging machines. He's written a whole scenario in his head. All of August off from work. A huge house all to himself. Free booze. In the mornings he'll swim in the pool and lie out in the sun and put on music and drink colorful cocktails. In the afternoons he'll walk the dog and water the lawn and flowerpots and then lie down again by the swimming pool and wait for Effie. Glamour. Hollywood. No one would believe him if he told them. And as soon as Effie gets off work she'll come straight there and they'll swim in the pool and then cook dinner and drink wine and do lots of other things, too – all night every night. Every night they'll stand naked across from one another and let their bodies go free and their bodies will approach one another slowly and hesitantly and slowly and hesitantly come together. Their bodies will rest on one another and their eyes will be closed and they'll smell one another and feel that strange thing. That heat that emanates from a body that's free of clothes. The sweetness and dizziness and desire born of the union of bodies. That's what he wants more than anything. The union of bodies. That's the gift he'll give to Effie, along with all the rest. And he doesn't care that it's only temporary, that it'll all be over in a month. He doesn't care that this life will end in a month. Because what someone once said – that the meaning of life is that it ends – is the only thing worth knowing, for however long you're fated to live. That and nothing else.

The meaning of life is that it ends.

And at the end of the month he'll get four hundred euros for his trouble.

Though he isn't actually so sure about that.

. . .

And then there's the dog.

Look after Leben like you would your own eyes, Alamanos said the last time he had him come to the house. Like your eyes. You hear?

They were sitting by the pool drinking whiskey on ice. The dog stood between his owner's legs and stared at him the whole time. Black eyes jet black blacker than you would believe. And whenever he reached out a hand to pick up his glass or light a cigarette, the dog threw its ears back and growled as if it were a toy – as if it were a mechanical dog and some gear inside it had broken.

The wife will write it all down for you, Alamanos said. About his food and walks and shit and everything. And the vet's phone number in case something happens, knock wood that it doesn't. So don't drop the ball on this one. You hear? I don't have two kids and a dog, I have three kids. Got it? Like your eyes. If anything happens to him. Got it? That's all I have to say. Like your eyes.

He stared at the dog, which was staring at him. He could hear Alamanos talking but his mind was somewhere else.

At some point the conversation came around to money and he thinks he said something to Alamanos about money. He thinks Alamanos said he would pay him but he isn't sure. Three or four hundred euros. He thinks that's what he said it but he isn't sure. He can't remember very well. He was still reeling from all the talk and the dog's growling and the booze and the evening heat and the lights reflecting off the water of the pool that gave the water a peculiar color, an exotic color that made him feel even more a stranger in that house, that life. He may have said it but he isn't sure. But if he didn't say it then, he's sure to at the end of the month. Alamanos is sure to give him something. For sure. Four hundred euros. Maybe not that much but something.

But he didn't tell Effie any of that.

. . .

It's almost eight when he gets to the house. He parks and turns off the engine and looks at the view from up there. Korydallos Neapoli Maniatika. You can see as far as the port and the sea and the islands. He looks at the view and thinks of Effie – of the nights he'll spend with Effie. August. Another whole month. The meaning of August is that it ends.

Then he brings his hands close to one another and stretches

out his thumbs. He holds his breath then lets it out slowly and lets his fingers relax and watches as they approach one another slowly and hesitantly and –

And then he hears the barking.

The dog has wedged its head between the bars of the front gate and is tossing its head and barking like mad.

Leben! Leben!

He gets out of the car and walks across the street and over to the gate, terrified.

Leben, hey guy. It's me, Leben. It's fine, it's just me. Lebenako. Down. Down, calm down.

The dog backs up a few steps and stands there stock still. It stands there and stares at him with its head cocked to one side. Black eyes, shiny white teeth. A tongue red as blood. Its fur blacker than ever. It does a circle around itself, then another, and then it stands there without moving at all. Then suddenly it lunges forward and crashes into the gate again. It's shaking all over, biting the bars of the gate, barking loud enough for three dogs.

Shut up. Fuck you and your Belgium too. Shut up.

He licks his lips then bites them and scans the area with his eyes. There isn't a soul in the street and no one seems to be at home in any of the houses. He takes the keys out of his pocket and tries to find the right one. His hands are shaking. And his legs. He's shaking all over. He takes a step forward with the key in his hand. The dog goes nuts. It growls, throws itself against the gate, bites the air.

Leben. It's me. Calm down. It's me, man. Did you forget me already?

. . .

He backs away from the gate and starts walking alongside the wall. As he walks he keeps his eyes raised, scanning the pieces of sharp glass glinting on top of the wall, looking for who knows what. He turns the corner and keeps walking. It's just not fair. Alamanos told him the dog would be chained up. He's sure about that – he remembers it clearly. But now the dog is loose and is barking and throwing itself against the gate and biting the bars like it wants to break them in half. How the hell is he going to get in there? It's unfair. Unfair.

If only he had something to drink. Something to drink, to get his courage up.

He pulls the piece of paper out of his pocket and unfolds it and reads what it says. His hands are still shaking. They're sweaty, too. If the temperature stays under 38 degrees he can water every other day. If it goes above 38 then he needs to water every day. If the alarm goes off he presses this button – the bitch wrote a huge list of this shit. Temperatures codes telephone numbers. But not a word about what to do if the fucking dog goes nuts.

Around the other side of the wall he finds a green metal door. He doesn't remember Alamanos showing him that. He checks to see if it's open but it's locked. He looks again at the sheet of paper and then folds it up and stuffs it in his pocket. He tries one of the keys in the door. Then another. Before he can try a third he hears the barking getting louder. It's close, right on the other side of the door. Then the dog stops barking and there's another sound behind the door, a terrible sound, a sound like he's never heard before.

He shudders.

He looks up and down the street. Not a soul. A thousand things are passing through his head. It's unfair. It's just unfair.

And then he kicks the door as hard as he can.

The pain shoots up his leg to his stomach and chest and throat. He hops on one leg and his eyes tear up with pain. Incredible pain. He thinks he hears something from behind the door, something like panting, but he isn't sure.

Years ago he used to get it on with a girl from Nikaia. Olga. From a good family, she was a student at the nuns' school in Piraeus. Her mother didn't like him and made her break it off. And when they went on vacation – it was summer, August, same as now – he broke into her house one night. He'd been drinking all afternoon and at night he broke into the house with a bottle of cheap whiskey and sat on the sofa and imagined all kinds of things. He was drunk, blind drunk. He imagined that he had a pocketknife and slit open all the cushions on the sofa and then all the mattresses and pillows in the house. He spray painted the walls and the mirrors, clipped all the wires, slashed clothes and tore up books, broke trays plates knick-knacks. He imagined shoving a rag deep in the toilet and another in the bathroom sink. All night he drank and imagined. But in the end he didn't do anything.

Except before he left he went into the bathroom and turned on the tap in the sink. That was all.

And now he'd like to do the same thing if he could. Go into the house and drink and then break things and tear things and leave the place filthy. He would piss in the fridge and cupboards and on all the beds. And the dog – he'd leave it for last. If only. If only he could do all those things and then run off to someplace far away. Forget the apartment the car his job and disappear like one of those black tornadoes you see on television that come out of nowhere, destroy everything, and vanish again. Only he doesn't want to lose Effie. He wants for them to stand naked at night in that enormous house and pretend it's theirs, pretend that they're people who aren't afraid or worried about money and work. People who have shaken themselves free from the meaning of life and from the creeping passion for things, things they don't have and will never have. And peaceful and fearless they'll let their bodies lean on one another and peaceful and fearless they'll feel the dizziness that's born of the union of bodies. That's what he wants. The union of bodies.

He limps away from the door and limps along the wall. His foot has swollen inside his boot, his palms are shriveled, sweat is dripping into his eyes. And though he no longer hears any barking he knows that the dog is also walking along on the other side of the wall. And when he gets back to the gate Leben is already there and jumps up onto its hind legs with its front paws on the bars and starts barking again and biting the air. Foam like white blood drips from its mouth and there's a crazed look in its dark eyes.

He looks at the dog. He looks at the sharp green glass on top of the wall. And above that the sky spreading itself endlessly out in the pitiless light of August.

I have something to say, he says.

But there's no one there to listen.

. . .

He gets into the Nissan and rolls down the window and looks at the dog that's stopped barking and is staring at him with its mouth hanging open and its ears pricked. It's laughing at him. It's watching him and laughing. It's clear as day, the dog is laughing. A laughing Belgian sheepdog. Belgian shitdog. Belgian shit-eating dog.

He lights a cigarette and leans his head back. His foot is numb and has started to swell inside his boot. He can feel the pieces of broken glass on the top of his head but he doesn't want to touch them.

He'll wait. He'll wait. Something will happen. At some point the dog will get tired and go off somewhere. It'll get hungry, or thirsty, or go to sleep. And as soon as that happens, he'll let himself into the house. And then he'll do something.

He'll wait. He'll sit all night in the car and wait. He'll wait for the whole night to pass. He'll stay there all night and the next day and as many days as it takes. He'll wait.

The swollen orange sun disappears behind the mountain. Night is falling. The glass on the top of the wall isn't glittering anymore. A bird flies over the wall and vanishes as if the sky swallowed it up.

He'll wait.

It's still only the third of August.

Go Out and Burn Them

MARCH EIGHTH, a day of wind and no sun. Through the kitchen window I watch as my father hangs clothes in the yard. He lifts them out of the basin shakes them out and clips them to the line with clothespins. Since Sunday after the memorial service and the hassle of relatives coming and going he's set himself to washing all of my mother's clothes – he won't leave a single stitch unwashed. Skirts shirts nightgowns. Winter and summer clothes. He's even washing her underwear. I thought he was doing it to kill time, to keep himself occupied, so he wouldn't think, wouldn't remember. But now I see him hang a cream-colored bra on the line and then a pair of panties with a little kitten on the front wearing a red bow – I see him standing there for a moment caressing that printed kitten with his thumb and I don't know what to say.

If only the kitchen had no window so I wouldn't have to see.

. . .

When I got there we drank coffee and smoked a cigarette. We didn't say much. How things are going at work, if I'll be able to get some vacation time around Easter – that sort of thing. Then I asked about the recycling. The blue bins the municipality set out in the neighborhood and the bags they distributed for people to collect aluminum cans and plastic containers. Oh, that, he said. Keratsini, riding the wave of progress. Mark my words, soon they'll be recycling people, too. Why not? After all, don't they already treat us like garbage? I wanted to bait him a bit more, see what he'd say about what happened the other day, but he pretended not to know what I was getting at, he didn't even mention it. At some point he pulled a packet of stamped letters held together by a thick rubber band out of his coat pocket and laid them on the table.

I found these yesterday afternoon in the attic. I had no idea she had them hidden up there. I stayed up all night reading them. We were married forty-three years and she never said a word. Take a look if you like, it's something to pass the time. They really threw me for a loop.

What kind of letters are they? I asked. Love letters?

He lowered his head and looked at me over his glasses.

No, he said. Nothing to do with love. All the love stuff I've put in the wash.

He ground out his cigarette in the ashtray, licked his finger and tapped a speck of ash off the table and flicked it into the ashtray, too.

If we'd gone to Germany we could have saved her, he said.

You remember what the oncologist said. Put a hundred thousand in your pocket and go to Germany. Sure, a hundred thousand. As if he were talking about drachmas, not euros. He had no idea. And the banks haven't caught on, either, have they? They should be giving out cancer loans. The way it's mowing people down they'd be making money hand over fist.

What are you talking about, Dad? Have you lost it completely?

I know exactly what I'm talking about. It's what to do that's beyond me.

He stood up and emptied the ashtray into the trash, rinsed it and set it upside-down in the sink. Then he took the basin of wet clothes and the basket of clothespins and went outside.

. . .

I make more coffee then sit down and take the rubber band off the packet and spread the letters out before me. They're mostly from the '60s, but a few are even older. Letters my mother wrote to her parents in Crete. Letters from her brother Drakos to their father. Letters between the siblings – my mother was one of six. Other letters from friends and relatives. Most are difficult to read – the ink is faded in places or the paper has stains or little holes as if mice have been chewing on them. I choose one at random and try to make out what it says. As I read, I keep coming across little gems, unexpected turns of phrase of the sort people wrote back then in their letters, in the good old days when the postman brought actual mail and not just bills and ads and notices about unpaid bills.

November, 1963. My uncle Drakos writing to his family.

Piraeus 11/27/1963

Dear honored Father and cherished Mother and beloved siblings. I received your dear brief letter and was very happy that you are well as we are too. Well father thank you very much for the basket everything was very nice the greens had rotted so we threw them out and they are gone to the devil the myzithra was moldy but Lefteria cleaned off the bad part grace be to God we ate it already and wish there were more.

Well father how is the weather in Vatolakkos. We here grace be to God have had plenty of rain it's been a harsh winter with lots of rain and everyone is sick with a cold Lefteria caught the Asian flu and didn't go to work yesterday well father love and health that is what is most important in life.

Well father and mother we finally got jobs on the busses I'm a ticket collector and now that I'm full-time I don't have to worry and everyday I thank the Virgin Mary for helping me I even get a day off every week and vacation.

Well father like all of Greece I was very upset about that great man of Democracy that man of freedom who was killed, all of Athens and Piraeus sigh with grief, every day on the bus all the people say what a pity and sigh these few things I write to you of that Sainted Man Kennedy.

I have good news also, I think we are headed for new elections. Well father you should know that the Center will win pay no heed to the newspapers that say Karamanlis has so much support those are photographs from 1961, they're not real and you can be sure that THE CENTER WILL WIN.

Well father I ask you to please send some olive oil, here I have to buy it and it's difficult I don't have much money to spare it's a shame for us in the capital to be asking like beggars for a little oil but if you can believe it I make 60 drachmas a day and spend 50 on food I work all day just to eat, this is all I write to you.

Mother please tell brother Stelios the hero of Olympiakos that when I come I'll bring him a ball and a uniform but I want him to learn to read and write tell him no more wasting his time. Hello brother Stelios Cretan hero of Vatolakkos you'll live forever and always be a fan of OLYMPIAKOS down with Panathinaikos Stelios my hero we beat Panathinaikos and from their grief Michalis and our uncle Giorgis didn't eat for two days they were so heartbroken.

Well father I learned you have a rifle and go out hunting so send us please a fowl.

Well mother I will come at Christmas but before I come I will have to see the beautiful bride father take care that *the girl is pretty and from a good family. Take care that nothing goes awry.*

Dear father and mother if I had money I would send you 200 drachmas for a cigarette.

I write you these few things and send kisses to you all and await your response. Give my regards to the neighbors and to anyone who asks after me. I await your letter. Your son Drakoulis.

. . .

At the bottom of the pile I find several letters from America. My mother's godmother had sent them from Nea Iorki, Broukli, Atlant Siri. It takes a while for me to figure out that the last is Atlantic City. They span just about a decade, from September 1958 to March 1967. As I flip through the pages Christmas cards and black and white photographs slip out from between the sheets, yellowed with age and of people I don't recognize at all. I find an undated postcard, too, showing a big white ship, the Olympia, with three bands of color on its funnel: yellow on the bottom, then blue, then black on top. The blue band has a yellow emblem painted on it that looks like a star on a stem. On the back of the card are printed the words *Greek Line – T.S.S. Olympia*. Beneath, several lines that are almost impossible to read, as if they'd been written by someone with Parkinson's.

*My dear relations we borded the boat from America on
March 12 eager to see you we arrived Lisbon today we have
a terrible sea I am in bed all the time with injections to stop
the vomiting the ships hospital is full of wounded people broken arms and heads Markoulogiorgenas's girl broke her knee
you wouldnt believe what we are going through waves like
mountains hit our boat people cry and pound there chests
I will write to you in detale from Athens when we reach there
my husband Fotis regrets it he says Virgin save us that is all
I write with love your koumbara Eleni Varipatakis.*

. . .

It's almost two. I get up and pour myself a tsikoudia, put a few
pistachios on a plate. My father is done with the laundry and
now he's wearing these orange plastic gloves and has gone over
to the building site across the street and is filling the municipality's recycling bags with plastic cups and papers. It's about
your father, Dina said the other night when she called. He's not
doing well, child. He wanders around the neighborhood picking
up trash from the street and throwing it in that cycling thing,
whatever it's called. Then this afternoon he tried to climb into
the bin. Jesus Christ in heaven, child. Stefanos was coming
home from work and caught him just in time. Barba-Tasos,
he says. Hey, barba-Tasos, are you nuts? What are you doing,

you're trying to get into the trash bin? Stefanakos, your father says, any man who lets his wife die like that deserves to go out with the trash. They can pick me up and recycle me, maybe I'll come out a more useful man. You hear that? Have you ever heard such a thing? Then he just sat there by himself and laughed. Child, things aren't right with your father. They're not at all right, and I'm telling you now so you'll do what you can. Because he's a good man who's had a tough time and everyone in the neighborhood feels for him.

The wind outside is stronger now. My mother's clothes are whipping around on the line. A blouse with embroidery on the sleeves, her green jacket, a flower-print dress with narrow straps. Clothes that look like they've never been worn, clothes that no one will ever wear again. A tin can rolls into the middle of the street. My father crushes it with his foot, tosses it into his sack then goes over to the blue bin. He empties the sack and stands in front of the bin with his arms at his sides. I close my eyes. I wait. I count to ten. To twenty. When I open them I see him standing at the gate looking at me in confusion, his mouth half open.

. . .

The longest letter is from Atlant Siri, dated 4/27/61. It caught my eye right away not only because it was the longest but also because it was the only one in an envelope. A clean blue envelope tied with a red bow, like a package. Like a wedding invitation.

Dear Lefterio my golden girl I got your letter and was very happy and please forgive me for not ansering right away. I was happy about the progress our Vatolakkos has seen and all the things you've written about that have made your lives easier God willing next year my husband Fotis and I plan on coming since he wants to get to know Crete we will stay 2 or 3 months and then leave again.

And when I go to the fields where I used to look for radishes I can go by taxi now that they've built roads since these days I cant imagine walking Ive reached a weight of 180 pounds. Grace be to God we are all well write to me how the olives are doing is there a good harvest this year? How is everyones work going? Are the oranges selling well? Tell my dear relation your mother to please leave me one orange tree with some oranges on it unsold so if the Virgin wills for us to come we can eat fresh oranges which I have missed so much. And please ask her to plant squash in my garden and when I come I can gather the squash greens and cook them with black nightshade to eat because that is the only dish Ive been dying for here Lefterio since in America you cant find squash greens or nightshade either. They bring zucchini from California but by the time it gets here its so mushy it turns your stomach to look at it.

I saw Lefterio what you wrote to me about your aunt Stella that she and her husband left for Argentina but that was a mistake. Things are much better in Athens than in Argentina where great poverty has fallen the whole place is poor it would have been much better for them to go to Canada than to go there they will regret it and wont stay long before they leave. Poverty is a terrible thing my Leferitsa here too we have many expenses I have my son Thodoris in California studying at the university who needs 2,000 dollars a year and it will take him 4 years to finish so Stella did wrong to go to Argentina but thats how it is so many people talk of leaving Greece and its best for them to go anywhere at all they might as well go anywhere since there is poverty all over now even here in America many people are without jobs and stay home and live off the state which is why it is so hard today for a person to imigrate to America because things are not too good and every year there are fewer jobs and so Ill stop there.

On Saturday my husband and I went to see Eftychia Karatzakis and stayed there most of the day. She and her husband will leave on May 20 to go home to Crete. I asked her if I could put together a little package I begged her a thousand times but she said no because she says she has too many things and cant take anything else. In the end I started crying and asked if I could send at least one little dress a dress for my Lefteritsa who I love so much and she said yes and so I am sending you a dress Lefterio so you can wear it on the feast day of Agios Pavlos and go to church and remember your godmother who is in foreign lands.

I saw Lefterio that you wrote to me that I should take care to find you a husband even if hes old so that you can come here. My sweet one just as a blind man wants to see the day so too do I want to bring my people here to save them from the troubles of Greece because its true that here it is a real paradise. But if imigration was open the way you write everyone would pack their bags and come to America not just from Crete but from the whole world. Ever since I came I have been trying to bring my brother Spiros and havent been able yesterday I went again to the imigration office with my husband Fotis and they told me I have to be married for 3 years to have the right as an American to invite some-one. And my aunt Maragkoudaina in Koufo asked me to make a place for her granddaughter Athina in my home and I answered her that I cant and my aunt got angry and stopped writing to me. There are strict laws Lefterio because if it was that way all of Greece would pack its bags and come here. I know my dear that life is very dramatic like you write to me and that your heart hurts and I tell you my heart hurts

229

too because I love you so much my good little girl which I know you are and I know you deserve a good fate my dear sweet good girl but I think you will understand that I have only been here a short while and I am not yet an American. The law says that I have to be married to an American citizen for 3 years in order to invite one of my own people here.

Lefterio please do not be sad I beg you. I beg you please do not do anything silly of the kind you write to me because it is a shame and unjust to God for a golden girl like you to have her heart poisoned like that. God is great my Lefteria. Be patient thats all I write to you.

I send greetings to everyone from my husband Fotis and from all my children give all my greetings to my relations your parents and to all your brothers and sisters and may we meet soon and please give my greetings to everyone and to all the neighbors and anyone who asks after us.

Goodbye and as a gift from me your godmother Eleni Varipatakis in my next letter I will send you a memento two dollars to remember me and to buy yourself a pensil.

. . .

My father comes into the kitchen. He sets the basin on the table and takes off the orange gloves and washes his hands at the sink. Then he sits and smooths his hair which the wind had mussed and reaches for one of my cigarettes. His hands are shaking, his palms are red and wrinkled. Who knows how many loads of wash he did again today.

I'm making lamb chops, he says. And Dina from next door brought pastitsio. I'm not eating meat but I'll boil some greens.

But he doesn't get up from the chair. He sits with his elbows on the table twirling the lit end of his cigarette against the ashtray and staring at the letters spread before him.

I get up and pour another tsikoudia and look out the window. I can see the cream-colored bra and the panties with the kitten on them fluttering on the line. It occurs to me to ask if they were a present from him. Because I can't imagine my mother going into a store and buying something like that. Panties with a kitten on them. Jesus. I certainly can't imagine her wearing them. Panties with a kitten. A kitten with a red bow. My mother.

Did you read them?

He stubs out his cigarette and sweeps the pile of papers over to his side of the table and starts to neaten them.

Not all.

On the very top of the pile is the postcard with the ship. He grabs it and brings it up to his eyes then flips it over. He rests his glasses on his forehead and rubs his eyes with two fingers. He looks at the blue envelope with the red ribbon that I've set aside and the long letter from Atlant Siri. He picks up the ribbon and wraps it around his hand and ties a bow and then puts it in his coat pocket.

Did you read this one? he asks.

I did.

A thousand times better, he says. A thousand times better if she had left. They have good doctors there hospitals and machines and things. They don't just let people die like a dog in the vineyard. Of course not. America America, he sings. How right they are who say your streets are paved with dreams of gold.

He rubs his eyes again, harder this time. The refrigerator is making strange noises. Crick crack. As if there's something alive in there that wants to get out. I read the tiny letters on the freezer door. I read the brand of the stove and of the toaster and of the clock on the wall. I'll look at anything to avoid my father's eyes.

Give me some of that.

He grabs my glass and takes a few sips. His Adam's apple slowly rises then sinks back down to its place.

He sets the glass on the table and then stands and picks up the basin.

I've got a load of dark clothes in the machine, he says.

In the doorway he pauses and pulls his glasses down off his forehead and looks at me.

I didn't know she wanted to go to America. What does it say in the letter? *You wrote that I should find you a husband even if he's old.* She was sixteen years old. You know? Just a girl, sixteen years old. And she wanted to get married even if the groom was old. I never knew. I swear to you. She never said a thing to me. Forty-three years together and she never said a thing. Other people did, though. Sure. I heard from other people. We all take a secret with us to the grave. Big or small everyone has one. People told me but I didn't believe. Impossible, I said. Lefteria and I won't ever have secrets. Not in life and not in death, either. That's what I said. Big words, sure. But I believed it. God knows I believed it. And now what'll happen, can you tell me that? How are we supposed to live now.

He turns his head and looks at the letters splayed out over the table. His eyes seem so small and red behind his glasses. Two strange creatures staring petrified at the world from behind a glass wall.

Burn them, he says. Go out and burn them. Don't throw them in the recycling. In a hundred years if the world still exists people will know everything about us and how we live now. Have you ever thought about that? How in a hundred years there won't be any such thing as the past. Who am I kidding, a hundred. It'll happen way faster. Sure. Time will be an endless present. Ever thought about that? Even our trash will still be around. That's why we have to destroy whatever we can while we can. Memory without gaps isn't memory. It's death. Go out and burn them. Just don't get any ash on the clothes out there. My back hurts from bending over the bathtub. Mind those clothes, you hear?

And then he leaves.

I pour another tsikoudia and drink it standing up in front of the window. Then I take a swig straight from the bottle.

I wonder if I should take my father to see a doctor.

I wonder what my mother did when she read that letter from Atlantic City.

I wonder if she closed her eyes and cried or if she forgot or if she kept on hoping. If that dress ever came if she wore it if she went to church. Whatever became of that dress, I wonder.

Outside the whole world is letting loose. The windowpanes are shuddering, the wind whistles through whatever crack it can find. My mother's clothes are whirling on the line like captive ghosts struggling to escape.

I wonder if that memento ever arrived.

If those two dollars ever came from America, if my mother ever bought that pencil.

People Are Streinz

SEVEN MONTHS without a single dream. Seven whole months. The twenty-first of May was the last time I had a dream. I remember because it was also the last time it rained around here. And I remember because it was Lena's name day and I said it was a good sign that it rained and I finally had a dream for the first time in a long time. But I haven't since then. And it hasn't rained again, either. No rain and no dreams. Dead silence.

Dreams and rain. Who knows. Maybe they go together these days.

Lena doesn't care about the rain. She doesn't care that it's almost Christmas and it's still twenty degrees outside. She doesn't care that everyone's walking around in short-sleeved shirts and outside the birds are singing like it's April. She doesn't care about dreams, either.

I don't dream, she says. I'm better off without dreams. What good did dreams ever do me? I just have the same one all the time, that I'm falling off a cliff and there's no one to catch me.

Why sit there worrying about stupid dreams. You've got plenty else to worry about. Yesterday they called again from the appliance place and asked about our payments. We're three months behind and this and that is going to happen if they take us to court. Did you hear? To court. Can you believe it? The guy had this tone of voice like he was talking to I don't know who. I wanted the earth to open up and swallow me whole. To have him humiliate me like that, and there was nothing I could say. And if we have to go to court they'll make us pay the lawyers' fees, too. Are you listening? Why don't you worry about that for a change. About stuff like that. Not dreams and rain.

She's holding a strip of orange peel and slicing it into pieces with a knife. She's already cut it into a thousand tiny slivers but she won't stop won't give up. She slices it into tiny pieces and then smaller ones and even smaller than that. A thousand slivers. And she's still at it.

Watch it, I say. The last thing we need is for you to lose a finger.

The twenty-first of December. Saturday afternoon. Four days until Christmas. Out the kitchen window I can see colored lights blinking on and off on the balconies and in the windows and yards of nearby apartments and houses. Red green yellow blue. Stars and garlands and Saint Vassilises and sleighs pulled by reindeer. An incredible number of lights. Like you're in an endless casino and all the houses are slot machines. Cement, poverty, and colored lights – Bangladesh meets Las Vegas. Kids are riding their bikes in the street and women are watering flowerpots full of bushy plants. I see men in shorts grilling meat and drinking beer on the rooftops of apartment buildings. I see a bird circling in the air around a birdcage and the bird inside flaps its wings too but in a surprised kind of way. The sky is completely clear, the air as dry as the mouth of a person who's very scared. Just a few days before Christmas but nothing looks like Christmas. Except for the lights. It's as if Christmas came and went and now it's spring but for some crazy reason everyone forgot to take down their decorations.

A few days before Christmas and something in the air around me is burning like a slow fuse. I wonder. I wonder when the fuse will burn down to the end and when the explosion will come and what will happen after that.

The other day I caught myself standing in front of a shop that sells hunting gear looking at the knives and switchblades in the window. Then I went in and bought a Buck knife, one of those American knives with a blade twenty centimeters long. It's no joke it's the real thing it can do some serious damage the heft of it in your hand makes your mind go dark. I carry it in my boot just in case, as they say. I didn't tell Lena about it. But at night when I can't sleep my mind wanders to things like that. Fuses and explosions and guns and knives. And I wonder what the hell is happening and where it's all heading. It scares me.

And then there's Lena dicing orange peel at the kitchen table. Slicing it silently with a knife in an utterly silent house. A silence like you wouldn't believe, like what they say about the silence before an earthquake. And I think about how if there's an earthquake maybe the weather will change, maybe it'll rain and get cold and maybe even snow. If there's an earthquake big enough to shake the whole world maybe something will change. And it scares me to be thinking those kinds of thoughts. What kind of life can you live without anything good, I say to myself.

What kind of life can you live when you're waiting for something bad to save you from something bad.

· · ·

There's half a bottle of wine left from yesterday. I fill a glass with feigned indifference, as if it were water, and Lena looks at me and starts to say something but I beat her to it.

Monday, I say. On Monday when I get my Christmas bonus I'll pay off the rest of what we owe at Kotsovolos. Okay?

Fine, she says. That's great. I can stop worrying.

She grabs another piece of orange peel and starts to slice it with the knife. Her fingers are yellow.

Do you maybe, just maybe, have some idea of how much we owe? she asks me. Take a piece of paper and start writing. Two months of building fees is two hundred euros. The car insurance expired on the fifteenth. That's another two hundred.

238

Rent. Kotsovolos. A hundred and forty to the electric company. The fucking credit cards from the fucking bank of fucking Cyprus. I have two cavities that need filling. By the time I'm forty I'll have no teeth at all. Who knows how much the dentist will cost. Why aren't you writing? You should be writing. And if you add it all up you'll see that to make ends meet we need the Christmas bonus and the Easter bonus and the bonuses for next Christmas and next Easter too. Write it. Write it down.

I grab the knife from her hands and throw it in the sink. She looks at me as if I were a stain on a white shirt and then opens the drawer and takes out another knife and goes back to cutting the peel right where she left off. Her fingers are yellow and trembling.

Lena, I say.

Write, she says.

. . .

I look out the window. The sky. There's a strange color in the sky again this evening. A gray like the underside of a piece of cardboard. Endless gray. No sun no moon no stars. Neither day nor night.

Not the sky but the underside of the sky.

Lena is on her second glass and second orange, peeling it and slicing the peel into tiny slivers which she lines up at the edge of the table. Her nails are yellow. The knife is yellow.

Even the table is yellow. I wonder whether I should go and get my new knife and sit across from her and start slicing orange peels, too. To take my mind off things. So I don't have to see that sky that's the color of clouds without actually having a single cloud in it at all.

I'll ask Vassilis for a loan, she says.

Which Vassilis? The saint?

A thousand. For the stuff that won't wait. Then we'll see.

A thousand? Are you crazy?

Calm down, he's your brother. If you can't ask your brother for help who can you ask. Sonia's offered a hundred times. Whenever you need, she said. We're doing just fine, she said. They're going to Paris for New Year's, did you know that? To Disneyland. They wanted to go to the Asterix village but it's closed in winter. It opens in March or April I think. She said they'll go to Jim Morrison's grave.

She stops slicing and looks out the window. A piece of white stuff from the orange is stuck to her chin, hanging there like a tiny thread over an abyss.

Jim Morrison, she says. That was so long ago. I use to love him when I was younger. I was completely in love. Crazy, passionate love. *People are streinz. People are streinz ouen yioura streinzer faces louk agli ouen yiouralon.*

She sings in a sweet husky voice and slices the orange peel and her voice as she sings sounds like a lullaby in the silence of the house and I think how I'd like for us to go to sleep and sleep for whole hours whole days and when we wake up it would be evening and raining and we would drink hot cocoa with cinnamon and eat grape must cookies with sesame seeds and then go out onto the balcony and smell the rain and the wet earth and there wouldn't be any knives or fuses or rent or debts – all those things will be gone and we'll have woken up new strange people with no nostalgia for anything. Nostalgia. A mangy dog with gunk in its eyes licking its wounds. It tricks you into reaching out to pet it then bites you as hard as it can.

I lean over and pluck the orange pith from her chin and roll it into a little ball and toss it into the sink.

Monday, I say. I'll take care of it all on Monday. Myself. No Vassilises and no Sonias. Okay?

She looks at me and then looks away.

I never expected this, she says.

What do you mean?

Nothing.

Tell me.

Nothing.

Then she cuts herself. The knife slips and cuts her on the thumb. But she doesn't say anything doesn't make a sound. She lets the blood run, looks at it calmly and indifferently the way brave people do on television. I go to grab her hand but she pulls away. She licks the blood, sucks at it then takes a paper napkin and wraps it around her finger. She looks at me with pursed lips and squeezes the napkin around the wound and the napkin turns redder and redder and then black.

Let me see, I say. Lena. It's me. We're not enemies. It's just me.

But she's looking at me as if I were the knife.

. . .

On Christmas Eve it seems like I'm having a dream. I say seems like, because for a long time I've been seeing things at night when I'm in bed and even though they seem like dreams I know they aren't because when I'm seeing them I'm awake. Of course I'm never quite sure anymore when I'm sleeping and when I'm awake. It seems to me that those two things have become one – or nothing at all. I'm sure the weather is to blame. It hasn't rained in seven months and now it's December but outside it's spring and the sun is as hot as two suns put together and every night I remember the winters we used to have and the cold and the rain and the snow. Some nights I get out of bed like a sleepwalker and open the cupboards and stick my head in the closet and smell the winter clothes and a sorrow like you wouldn't believe comes over me as I look at those winter clothes hanging in the closet and wonder if we'll ever wear them again or if they'll just hang there forever getting eaten by the dust and the mites, like ghosts of winters past, ghosts of a past life, our ghosts, the ghosts of us.

I dream that there's been a huge cataclysmic storm and the whole world is flooded and Lena and I are swimming in a strange place. We're swimming in a panic fighting for our lives and all around there's not a single soul in sight no houses no cars only water – black thick dirty water that sticks to us like something alive and scared. As I swim I hear Lena beside me saying that the water actually is alive and it's clinging to us because it wants to be saved from itself – that's what she says, saved from itself. The water wants to be saved from the water – that's the fine kind of dream I have. Then a huge tree appears before us with bare branches. I don't know what kind of tree it is but it's very big and there are lots of birds sitting in its branches – tiny red birds – and we see them flapping their wings in a panic but they can't fly. We swim very close and Lena says we have to help the birds fly away because the water level keeps rising and they're going to drown. But as soon as she grabs hold of one it vanishes and all that's left in her hands is a pile of feathers that aren't red but black. She grabs a second bird and then a third but the same thing happens – they vanish as soon as she touches them and she's left with a handful of black feathers. Then I try to grab one and my hands fill with black feathers and the water around us is getting blacker and blacker and rising higher and higher and weighing me down grabbing me and pulling me down down down.

Wake up, says Lena. What were you muttering, she says and shakes me. You scared me. Wake up.

She's leaning over me and in the dark her face is darker than the dark.

What were you dreaming? Why did you shout? What did you dream?

Nothing. Go to sleep.

What did you dream. Tell me.

Nothing. That it was raining. Go to sleep.

She falls back onto the mattress and sighs. Then there's no sound, only the tick tock of the clock. The sheet has wrapped itself around my legs and it's too tight but I don't have the energy to push it off.

See, Lena says. It's a good sign. See, you shouldn't lose hope. See.

Then she leans toward me again and puts her hand on my neck and kisses me on the side of my head.

· · ·

On Christmas Day the weather changes. Around noon the clouds come out and by three the sky is dark. Sonia calls to wish us a merry Christmas. They're in Pelion with friends. It's been raining since morning there, she says. Lots of rain, insane amounts of rain. I'll fill up a bottle and bring it to you, she says and laughs. They're all drunk, the whole stupid bunch of them. They're staying in a hotel whose restaurant has organic meats, organic vegetables, organic forks and knives. Their room has a fireplace and a four-poster bed with a canopy and walls painted all kinds of crazy colors. How nice for you, Lena says, looking at me. Then she asks Sonia when they're coming home, if they'll get to see one another before Sonia and Vassilis leave for Paris. I wanted to ask you something, Lena says – her eyes on me the whole time. About what we were saying the other day. You remember. Yes. No. I'm fine. For sure. We'll talk when you're back.

When she hangs up, we take our drinks out onto the balcony. It's going to rain. A tall cloud like a black wall is heading toward us from the direction of Salamina. It's going to rain. Only the wind doesn't smell like rain. It's a strange wind. Blowing from the east, from the opposite direction of where the cloud is, but the cloud is still moving steadily toward us. As if it isn't a cloud but something else. The power lines in the street hum, metal doors bang, car alarms shriek. Trees and TV antennas bend in the wind, which sweeps up leaves and plastic bags and scraps of paper. A star-shaped ornament pulls loose from a balcony and falls into the street and rolls like some strange wheel. The wind is fierce and blowing steadily toward the west as if the cloud is an enormous magnet put there to suck up everything in the world, to suck all the air out of the world.

Look over there, Lena says, grabbing my arm. What's that about, she says, pointing to the cloud. What on earth. Look. Have you ever seen anything like it? What is it?

And then we see the rain. Distant black threads hanging from the cloud that seem to tie the earth to the sky.

It's the end of the world, I say, and Lena laughs as if she can't breathe and clings to me and licks up a droplet of wine that dripped from her glass onto her hand.

Maybe this really is how the world will end, I say. Then again, maybe not. Maybe the world won't end, only the people. Maybe people will stop having dreams or sleeping or making love or drinking wine or kissing. Something like that. Maybe that's how the end will come. Not from meteorites or nuclear weapons or melting ice caps. No explosions or earthquakes or typhoons. Not from outside but from within. That's how it should be. Because we're living in the world but not with the world. For centuries now we've stopped living with the world. So it wouldn't be fair if the world had to end with us. It wouldn't be fair.

The cloud is so big now that we can't see the sea at all.

A fake fir tree gets blown off a balcony across the street and falls into the emptiness below, silently spinning. It's the most frightening thing I've ever seen in my life.

Actually, no, I say. The most frightening thing is work. Waiting to get paid on every fifteenth and thirtieth day of the month.

Measuring your life in fifteen-day chunks. Knowing that if your bosses don't feel like paying you once or twice or ten times in a row, ten fifteen-day chunks, there's not a damn thing you can do about it. Your whole life is in their hands. And there you are counting your life out in fifteens. That's the most frightening thing.

I'm going inside, Lena says. I hate it when you talk like that. I don't want to watch anymore. Let's go inside.

But we don't go anywhere. We stand there holding our drinks and silently watching the rain coming in from the west. We watch as that black curtain of rain slowly and silently closes in slowly and silently swallows up the shapes and colors and noises of the sunset to the west.

Penguins Outside
the Accounting Office

THIS MORNING MY father swallowed five tacks. Metal tacks – the big kind. As soon as he saw Petros coming through the door in handcuffs with a cop on either side he took the tacks out of his shirt pocket and swallowed them all at once. Like candies. He was sitting right next to me but I had no idea it was happening. I mean at some point I saw him fishing around in his pocket but how could I have imagined. I thought he had a pill in there or something. How could I have imagined. Because he hadn't given any sign. Last night when he came home he was calm – no shouting no breaking plates no nothing. Calm. Like a beaten dog. Calm. Of course he didn't sleep at all. He spent the whole night sitting in the dark in the kitchen. I got up twice and found him sitting there in the dark, staring out the window. One hand propped against his cheek the other messing around in the ashtray with his cigarette as if he were writing something in the ashes. Calm. Except for his foot tapping on the floor. Tap.

Tap. Tap. He was barefoot and I wanted to tell him to put on socks since the last thing we needed was for him to catch cold but I didn't say anything. I just went back to bed and listened for a long time to his bare foot tapping on the floor.

Tap. Tap. Tap.

As if he was listening to some music no one else could hear.

. . .

In the morning at the courthouse he was still calm. Hunched over and silent but calm. Until Petros appeared in handcuffs with the cops pulling him along. Five tacks. I didn't notice a thing. It all happened so fast in the blink of an eye as they say – like in a dream. He took the tacks from his pocket and swallowed them and it wasn't easy but he forced them down. And then he clutched his neck and crumpled to the floor and turned blue all over and might have been trying to say something but all that came out was a hrrrrr hrrrr and he was shaking all over with his eyes wide open like a dog that's been poisoned. Everyone ran over to him, people were shouting, they thought he'd had a heart attack or a stroke – all hell broke loose. Petros tried to run over, too, but the cops grabbed him and threw him down. You cocksuckers, he shouted at them. Let me go you motherfuckers that's my father. But they just held him pinned down with their knees on his back. Like he was some kind of terrorist, like Koufodinas from November 17th. I don't remember what happened next – I wasn't really seeing things too clearly at that point. I was drenched in sweat, dizzy, trembling. All I remember is the ambulance coming to take him away. And then someone came and leaned over and gave me a good look and asked the guy next to me:

What did this guy swallow? A screwdriver or something?

. . .

It's been about a month now. I'm sure it started earlier but it's been a month since I found out. When Petros got off work he would take the Cadet and park on Thebes Street and wait. He worked at Grekas's warehouses behind Plato's Academy and as soon as he got off work he would park the Cadet on Thebes Street and watch the cars go by. He would put on his hazards and smoke a cigarette and listen to one of the cassettes I had given him and roll down the window and watch the cars go by. When he caught sight of an expensive one – some convertible or huge jeep – he would start the engine and pull out and follow it. Piraeus Kastela Faliro however far they went. Glyfada Voula Ilioupoli, all those fancy suburbs down the coast. He followed the expensive cars because he wanted to see where the people driving them lived or worked. He would drive around for hours like an aimless curse. The night he told me about it he'd come home drunk and collapsed onto his bed with all his clothes on and lit a cigarette and sang a song by Robert Johnson – he didn't know the words so he could only sing the tune – and then he said it's strange to be poor, it's so strange to be poor, you're like one of those penguins they show on TV watching the ice melt all around them and they have no idea what to hold onto or how to keep themselves from going crazy and so they start attacking one another out of fear – that's what it's like, Petros said.

Then he stood up put his hands on his hips and started waddling through the room making strange noises and I got out of bed and switched on the light and said you're wasted again you idiot if he wakes up and sees you like this he'll kick you from here to tomorrow and Petros said leave me alone I'm doing my penguin routine and then he stopped and looked at me and said penguins are an endangered species you're not allowed to hit them so if anyone dares raise a hand against me I'll report him to the ecologists. When I turned off the light he stopped moving and lit a cigarette and looked out the window at the flickering lights of the ships down at the port and said that another Friday had come and gone and Grekas still hadn't paid them their wages.

He owes us two months of back pay, he said. We all lined up at four in the afternoon outside the accounting office, waiting. Fifteen or twenty of us. They paid the first five or six and the rest of us went home empty-handed again. I was eighth in line. We shouted and swore but we can't change the facts. Next week, he says. This old guy barba-Kostas who works the backhoe fainted when he heard. We ran over to try and help. There's nothing in the world more – what's the word. More humiliating than that. To not get paid for two months and to wait in line for your wages and when your turn comes they say sorry we ran out of money come back next week. It's sick. A sickness. Soul-destroying. You should have seen us. We were just like penguins. Waiting in line inching forward and stretching our necks out to see what was happening in the office and if the next guy to go in was getting paid or not. We were just like penguins, really. And the whole time we were waiting there it wouldn't have taken much for me to tear into the guy in front of me and I knew perfectly well that the guy behind me would have torn into me too. Because we all knew there wasn't enough money to go around. It would have made your blood freeze to see us like that. Like penguins, I swear.

. . .

I leave the hospital on foot because I don't have money for a cab but also because I feel like walking. Five tacks. The doctors say two of them are stuck in his esophagus and the others went down into his stomach. It's not going to be an easy case. He's over seventy and he's got heart problems. They're going to do something but they didn't tell me what. They might not even know themselves. They might not even want to do anything – who knows. They sent me home to get his pills so they'll know

253

what he's taking and I'm also supposed to bring his pajamas and slippers. They practically chased me out of the place and that makes me wonder, too.

It's December and there's a full moon and a clear sky and the breath comes out of my mouth like fog. Friday evening. They're going to keep Petros in jail all weekend – they'll bring him back to the courthouse on Monday. I called the lawyer from the hospital and he told me. It's like the junta, he said. We're living through another junta. They won't let him out on bail because he's a flight risk, they say. I never heard such a thing. Of course that brother of yours isn't an easy one. He's got guts, that's for sure. What was he thinking? A young kid like that. At any rate on Monday we'll get him out, no question. Patience, that's all I can say. It's only two days.

I turn left on Second Division, right on Heroes and end up out in front of the public theater where I think about taking a bus but keep on walking towards the port. Christmas. It's nearly Christmas and there are big fake candles flickering on the utility poles and garlands hanging over the street with fir trees and Saint Vassilises and reindeer. Up there it's Christmas but down here it's Good Friday – the sidewalk spattered with spots that look like blood as if someone came this way who'd been shot or some wounded animal left a long trail of blood behind. Dried black blood.

Last night they caught him in Glyfada. Petros. They caught him down in Glyfada. He'd waited again at Thebes Street and followed a jeep with a woman inside who was by herself. When they got to Glyfada and the jeep pulled into a garage Petros got out of the Cadet and went and looked over the fence and saw the most beautiful house he'd ever seen in his life – a huge villa as big as a castle and a yard with grass and trees and strange lights and in the middle a Christmas tree that seemed to be made of ice. Then, before the woman could close the garage door, Petros slipped inside and refused to leave. He didn't want to do anything didn't want to bother anyone. He just wanted to spend the night out there in the yard and look at the house and the grass and that strange tree that seemed to be made of ice. That's all he wanted.

But the woman and the house happened to belong to a judge, or a public prosecutor or something.

We heard it all from the lawyer – Petros didn't even call.

· · ·

On the corner of Georgiou and Resistance I have to wait for the light to change. The wind is fierce and a thick yellow frost coming from the port obscures the streetlights and the lights in shop windows. There seem to be even more stains on the sidewalk now, as if not just one wounded person but a whole army passed by.

The light turns red and I cross the street with my eyes on the asphalt.

He was yelling something about penguins, the lawyer said. It took them ages to calm him down. He was pretty wild, even tore one of the policemen's shirts. Completely wasted.

. . .

I stuff pajamas shirts underwear and socks into an overnight bag. I put whatever medicine I can find in a plastic bag. I pour myself a tsipouro to get warm – my hands are wooden with cold, my legs still shaking from the walk. And then I do something I haven't done in years: I stick the whole top half of my body into the hall closet and smell. When we were kids Petros and I used to do it all the time. In winter. We would sneak out into the hall at night and open the closet and slip inside to smell the clothes – ours, our father's, our mother's. Hers had a stronger smell than the rest. Walk on cotton so the cat won't catch you, Petros would whisper. I have no idea where he learned that saying. Walk on cotton so the cat won't catch you. We laughed so hard on those nights. And then we would go back to bed with the smell of the clothes lingering in our mouths and with that sweetness on our tongues we would fall asleep, arm in arm.

Things are different now. Other times, another house, other clothes – even the smell in the closet is gone. It seems to me that everything has lost its smell. Or maybe it's just me who lost those smells, who knows.

The heat is off and there's cold air coming in around the kitchen window. I stuff paper napkins into the cracks and push them down hard. Then I see the box of tacks sitting on the kitchen table.

I pour out another tsipouro and then open the box, take out a tack and put it in my mouth. It tastes bitter.

It's December and there's a full moon and a clear sky full of stars. I remember Petros telling me once that somewhere way back when, in Peru or maybe Mexico, people believed that humans were born from stars. Rich people had descended from a golden star and poor people from a bronze one. That's why they can't ever be equal. Because they were born into different worlds.

It really is strange, to be poor.

The wind is still whistling through the cracks. I look at the stars which from here all look the same – exactly the same, not gold and not bronze either. The tack feels cold in my mouth.

It must be cold where Petros is tonight.

Piece By Piece
They're Taking My World Away

THE WAVES FELL on the shore like shipwrecked men, broken-spirited, disheartened and weak, one after another, with clipped moans, small sighs, one after another. The squall had begun to die down in mid-afternoon and now the sun was shaping a huge burning hourglass over the calm waters which were full of seaweed and branches and pinecones and tin cans and plastic bags and broken fishcrates – thin bleached sticks like the bones of fish that had been eaten by bigger fish. But in the distance past the mouth of the bay the clouds had started to turn red again and to sink low over the sea, growing and growing until they once more snuffed out the horizon.

It was past seven but the machines were still at work – a hum rose from deep in the mountain's guts, disturbing the tranquility of the landscape. Eminent domain.

Look at that, he told her, pointing to the hourglass. If I had a boat I would take you to where the water becomes fire and you'd grab them both in your hands and hold them, the water and the fire too. Both together. Water and fire. Wouldn't that be nice?

Niki shooed a fly from her knee and threw her head back and looked upside-down at the cloud of dust rising between the blackened slopes of the mountain.

But you don't have a boat, she said. You don't even have an oar. You don't have anything.

He didn't reply. Eminent domain. He kept his arm stretched out – hand in a ball, index finger pointing – and let his mind wander to heroic thoughts. He imagined he was a warrior leading a troop of other warriors, pointing to the object of some daring mission, an enemy stronghold they had to conquer at all costs.

Sorry, Niki said. She turned to look straight forward again and stirred the ice in her drink with a finger and took a sip. I didn't mean it. That you don't have anything. I didn't mean it. You've got words, that's for sure. And imagination. Go on, I'm listening. What kind of boat would it be? Rowboat or sailboat? Motorboat? Tell me, I'm listening. How long has it been since you told me a story? Talk to me. Talk.

· · ·

They were sitting under the old olive tree in the garden drinking martinis out of plastic cups. That morning they had sent off

260

the last of their things by truck. All that was left was a single suitcase and an old mattress for them to sleep on that night, their last in the house. Eminent domain. They had been living in that house for five years. Five whole years. It was the nicest house they'd ever lived in, a real house, the kind they don't build anymore. There wasn't another like it in all of Salamina. Old, sure, but solid as a fort, with stone walls like ramparts, wooden beams, a tile roof, huge rooms – cool in summer, warm in winter – with fireplaces and a cellar and big windows that looked onto the sea. And around the house an enormous garden, an estate, really, with olive and orange trees, pine trees, and eucalyptus trees that on summer afternoons cast their shade over the low stone wall and in the sunny gaps between shade lizards lay motionless gathering sun to warm themselves, small ones and big ones, all of them green, salamanders and geckos with bulging eyes and long skinny tails.

Eminent domain. They were expropriating the property. The new road to the port on the far side of the island, behind the mountain, would pass through here. The guy who owned the place hadn't fought it at all. He didn't care. It was a lot of money and he lived abroad, he was a foreigner now, had emigrated to Belgium or Germany a long time ago, hadn't set foot on the island in years.

Eminent domain.

. . .

At night the locals came and took stones from the wall around the property. They came with pickup trucks and brought tools to loosen the stones and casually loaded them onto the beds of their trucks, slow and easy, taking their time. They were beautiful stones, big solid hand-chiseled slabs, they made you happy to look at and touch. The first night the locals came he yelled at them. Get lost, you buzzards, he shouted. You buzzards, you crows, aren't you ashamed? There are still people living here, get lost. Buzzards. Get out of here. He shouted and cursed and at one point it almost came to blows. But eventually he got tired of shouting and cursing and fighting. What was the point? What difference did it make, today or tomorrow. What was the point. A soul that's ready to leave will leave.

No use wasting our energy, he told Niki. We need to keep something in reserve for the future, for whatever's in store for us up there. It's a tactical move, see.

. . .

They were leaving for Kyustendil up in Bulgaria. A friend of a friend had opened a hotel up there and was looking for employees, he didn't trust the locals. He was looking for people he could depend on, without obligations, willing to work hard. The money was good. Good for Bulgaria, at any rate. They thought it over pretty hard, discussed it, and in the end said they'd give it a shot. He'd been the one to insist, he thought they should go. It's an opportunity, he told Niki. You see what's happening here. There's no way of getting ahead. It's over, we're over. It used to be that you worked your whole life for a bit of bread, now you work for a handful of crumbs. It's Bulgaria, sure, but that doesn't bother me. They say it's nice up there. Countryside mountains rivers forests. There are hot springs. And cherries. People say they grow the best cherries in the world up there. Lord, fresh cherries. And waterfalls, too. Here you can't even drink from the tap anymore. We spend fifty euros a month just on bottled water. It's over here, it's all over. You can't get ahead.

I say we go. It can't be worse than here.

. . .

Now, in the yard, he didn't respond. He reached down, tossed some ice cubes in his cup and filled it, then glanced at the hourglass that was rapidly shrinking and vanishing over the dark murky blue waters. He wasn't a warrior. A warrior fights to protect things he has and doesn't want to lose, or fights for things he doesn't have but wants to obtain. A warrior doesn't flee the field of battle to go and work for someone else. At a hotel. In Kyustendil, Bulgaria. Hot springs. Like Aidipsos, only in Bulgaria.

Niki closed her eyes, threw her arms back and stretched in her chair, then sat there as still as a gecko gathering sun to warm its cold blood. In the sunlight her armpits gleamed white and soft and smooth. He raised his sunglasses to his forehead and stared at her for a long time. He wanted to lick her armpits. Wanted to lick the sweat, which smelled of apples and salt, from her armpits. He wanted to suck up all the air between them and make it disappear, to demolish the distance between them, to destroy all the things that kept them apart.

In June he had killed a lizard. Sunday afternoon, a heat wave, he'd been sitting in the garden drinking just like now. He'd been picking up pebbles and tossing them at the lizards that had come out to sun themselves on the stone wall. He was throwing little pebbles at the salamanders for no real reason, just to pass the time. He wasn't thinking about what he was doing. He wasn't thinking about the pebbles or the lizards. He was daydreaming. He dreamed that they'd made lots of money and quit their jobs and bought this house and a brand new motorboat with a pointed prow and strong engine and they spent whole days out at sea – they rode around in the boat and fished and went to neighboring islands and swam and in the evenings as the sky grew dark they lay down in the prow and ate huge cold bowls of fruit salad – watermelon honeydew banana pineapple – and licked the salt tang off each other's bodies and lay arm in arm watching the red sun fading out in the distance and the little lights flickering on along the shore-lines of the islands and on the ships further out at sea – lay watching the stars appearing in the sky and there were so many of them and they were so far away that when he and she lay silently staring at those stars they felt a kind of pain inside. That was the kind of dream he was dreaming, dreams of a summer afternoon. And then without even realizing what he was doing he picked a bigger pebble up off the ground and threw it at the wall and the rock hit a lizard and killed it on the spot. He jumped to his feet, ran over, looked. A tiny green lizard with a long tail, identical to all the others. Motionless on the thick stone of the wall, a red spot between its eyes where the rock had landed. He poked it with a stick, blew on it, talked to it. Nothing. Just like that, quickly and simply, he had killed a lizard.

He looked around. There was no one there, nothing had changed, everything was the same as before, just as it always was, the trees the low wall the grass the flowers the house and inside the house Niki reading or sleeping and behind the house in the distance the sea the boats the ships the trash in the water the islands the people the world. Nothing had changed.

Quickly and simply.

As quickly and simply as god surely kills people all the time, tossing absentminded pebbles at the world, dreaming his own dreams.

. . .

They gave me a card at the bank, he said.

He put his sunglasses back on and looked at the hourglass over the water. It had shrunk by half and didn't look anything like an hourglass anymore.

Six thousand with no annual fees. So, I'll buy you a boat, he said. Nothing fancy but it'll do the job. We'll be fine making the payments. I'm not that useless, I can pay off a credit card. How does that sound? I'll find a place where we can leave it and in the summer when we come back here we'll have a new boat waiting for us. I'll start playing the lotto, too. I'm sure they have stuff like that up there, there's no place that doesn't have lotto. You'll see. I can't buy back all the years that have passed but I can buy you a piece of tomorrow. You'll see. It's enough if we're together and happy. Love and faith bring luck. You'll see.

She opened her eyes and looked at him sideways, then looked at his glass and at the bottle sitting by his feet. She laughed.

What did you say?

Nothing.

What'd you say?

Nothing.

But you said something.

. . .

At night the locals came and took stones from the wall around the property. They turned off the coast road climbed up the hill on the dirt road and stopped in front of the fence with their headlights trained on the fence so they could see what they were doing. They came with pickup trucks and brought tools to loosen the stones and casually loaded them onto the beds of their trucks, slow and easy, taking their time. They were beautiful stones, big solid hand-chiseled slabs, they made you happy to look at and touch. The first night the locals came he yelled at them. Get lost, you buzzards, he shouted. You buzzards, you crows, aren't you ashamed? There are still people living here, get lost. Buzzards. Get out of here. He shouted and cursed and at one point it almost came to blows. But eventually he got tired of shouting and cursing and fighting. What was the point? What difference did it make, today or tomorrow. What was the point. A soul that's ready to leave will leave.

No use wasting our energy, he said to Niki. It's a tactical move, see.

. . .

An idiot mayor, Niki said. You're talking like an idiot mayor. That's what I said. Like a priest and a mayor rolled up in one.

Love brings luck, huh? Okay, Father, whatever you say. Pour me another martini.

She held the bottle between her bare thighs opened it tilted her glass and filled it up to the rim then looked over his head at the cloud of dust rising from the far side of the mountain. Eminent domain. Day and night the workers and machines kept at it, gutting the mountain, opening a new road toward the port. Lately at night when they sat under the olive tree they thought they could still hear the echo of the hum of the machines thought they could see red dust falling onto the trees, onto the fence, onto their faces and hair. And when they drank or ate they thought they could feel dust in their food and drinks thought they felt dust in their mouths and throats. Dust. They ate dust drank dust coughed dust sweated dust.

Eminent domain.

Lately at night they'd been dreaming. Dreams of Kyustendil – if you could call them dreams. Confused, anxious, unfair dreams. The kind where you keep trying to do something, you struggle for what seems like hours to achieve something important, something beautiful, something that in your dream you know will change your life forever, but in the end you fail. That was the kind of dream they'd been dreaming, unfair dreams. And they woke in terror, bathed in sweat, thinking they could hear the other person's heart beating even louder than their own.

There were lots of times when he woke up screaming, and Niki would lean over and stroke his forehead his cheeks his chest.

Don't be scared, she'd say. I'm here. Don't be scared.

They would lie awake for a long time silently listening to the sounds of the night which was up as late as they were. The crickets and the cicadas. The rustle of the leaves and the sighing sea and all the sounds that frighten a person at night. The creaking of roofbeams, the hum of the fridge, a dripping faucet, something creeping along the floor or wall. Silently they listened to the night speaking around them and their skin crawled.

When day broke, much later, he said to her:

That's what love is. To have the same dream at the same time on the same night with the person who's sleeping beside you. Who'd believe it if you told them? The two of us are alone in the world. Even in sleep we're in love.

She looked at him in the dark, then turned over so she wouldn't have to see him anymore.

They're not dreams, they're nightmares, she wanted to say, but in the end she didn't.

. . .

The ice cubes had melted. He went to get some water from the fridge. Bottled water, a euro and sixty cents per six-pack. Fifty euros a month. Six hundred euros a year. For months now they hadn't been drinking water from the tap because it came out looking like rust. In the hall the plastic bottle slipped from his hand. His hands were shaking again. He walked past the old mattress leaning against the wall and went out and sat down on the cement.

I say we pull the mattress out here and sleep in the yard tonight, he said. It's our last night here, we should sleep in the yard. What do you say?

Niki shrugged.

Do whatever you want, she said. I won't be sleeping at all.

By now the hourglass was gone, the sea was darkening, a breeze had picked up. They sat for a long time under the olive tree listening to its leaves shudder in the wind. The stars trembled between the branches of the tree and he stared at them for a long time silently trying to think of what the stars looked like trying to think up something heroic, something romantic to say about the stars but in the end he gave up because they were only stars—they were only stars and nothing more.

. . .

Should I bring you a jacket or something? he asked.

Chuckwalla.

What's that?

Bulgarian. It means love brings luck. Chuckwalla. Isn't it nice? Say it: chuckwalla.

He gave her a quizzical look and Niki laughed and rubbed her forearms which were covered in gooseflesh.

I've been trying to remember since morning, she said. I've been trying to remember since when we were loading our things onto the truck and now I finally did. Chuckwalla. Turns out you were right, alcohol is an aid to memory. Wasn't it you who told me that? Anyway. Whoever said it was right. I feel like singing. There's no one to sing for us. No one to sing songs about us, the ones who are leaving now. Like the songs they used to sing in the old days. I know, you'll say a lot has changed since then. And you'd be right, too. Back then a guy could sing *at the station in Munich you left me* and now what's he going to sing, *at the station in Kyustendil you left me?* It just doesn't sound right. Besides, who knows if there's even a station up there. Are there trains in Kyustendil? Did you even ask? You didn't, did you. That's why no one is going to sing songs about us, the ones who are leaving now. But it's fine, I'm sure they'll say something on TV. That's something, at least. At some point they'll say something on TV for sure. About all the people who are leaving. I'm sure. Of course they will. That's something, isn't it? Better than nothing. Pour us another drink. I want to drink to the health of progress and development and eminent domain. To the health of the European Union and the free movement of people and products. Cheers to that.

He got up from the cement and stood in front of her.

Let's go inside, he said. Let's go in and lie down, okay? It's too windy out here, it's not a good idea for us to sleep outside. Come on. Get up, let's go in. Get up. We've got a big day ahead of us tomorrow.

Niki didn't look his way. She was staring at the clouds that were getting bigger and blacker and blocking out every part of the horizon. A lightning flash carved across the sky. It looked like an enormous uprooted tree.

You don't remember, Niki said.

What? What don't I remember?

The chuckwalla. That documentary we saw. About the lizards. You don't remember. There are these lizards in Mexico that when they get scared they hide in their nests and puff up their lungs with air so they're as big as balls and no one can get them out no matter how hard they try. They're called chuckwallas and I'm so jealous of them. I wish I could do that. The chuckwalla of Salamina.

He reached out a hand to touch her shoulder. Niki took a deep breath and puffed out her cheeks and held her breath until her face turned red and her eyes filled with tears and got blurry and she started to see little black flecks flitting before her eyes like tiny insects hovering over something that's died.

Then she let her breath out in a gust and, panting, let her red face drop to her chest.

Piece by piece they're taking my world away, she said.

. . .

Late at night she saw headlights coming along the coast road. She was curled up in her chair, trembling from the cold, but her jacket was in her suitcase and she didn't want to go inside to get it, she didn't want to wake him. She knew he would wake up on his own at some point during the night. She was sure to hear him shouting, on this last night in the house he would wake up shouting again from some dream. For sure. Eminent domain.

The truck turned left and started up the dirt road, growling up the hill, then stopped in front of the gate. The driver's side and passenger's side doors opened at exactly the same moment. The men stepped out and glanced into the yard. She couldn't tell if they saw her sitting there – but if they did, they showed no sign of it. They took something out of the truck and then came over to the wall and started to loosen the stones and load them onto the bed of the truck.

She curled up even tighter in her chair and wrapped her arms around her bare legs and in the darkness saw her skin filling with countless tiny goosebumps, countless blind eyes. Eminent domain.

She watched as the men walked back and forth through the

beams of the truck's headlights. They would work a stone loose from the wall and carry it to the bed of the truck and then come back for another. They worked calmly, without rushing, without fear. One of them said something and they both laughed and the laugh seemed to echo between the trees and the shadows of trees and Niki saw new eyes, blind eyes, sprouting from her skin.

And then, when they left, when the truck rolled back down the dirt road and went out onto the main road and disappeared, raising a cloud of red dust, Niki lifted her head and saw all the stars in the sky without really looking at any one of them – the stars are the sky's eyes, what a fairytale, the sky has no eyes it's blind blind blind – and she reached a hand toward the stars like a beggar and held her arm stretched out like that for a long time and when it got tired she lowered her arm and with it her gaze and she stared at the low stone wall, at the terrible gap those loosened stones had left in the wall.

Piece by piece they're taking my world away.